"I know what yo

"And what is that?" chance to have a few minutes alone with her.

Brooke turned to face him. Leaning against the fridge, she met his gaze and answered dryly, "The same thing I think when I see Cole looking at you like you're some kind of super hero. It's not enough reason for us to get together."

Nate set aside what he was doing and slowly crossed the distance between them. He stopped in front of her, and braced a forearm on either side of her slender shoulders.

He hadn't intended to make another move on her, here and now, but then he hadn't intended a lot of things when it came to Brooke Mitchell.

"Then how about this?" Nate offered softly. He watched her marine blue eyes widen as he leaned in to kiss her.

Dear Reader,

What makes a good father? To answer that question, I have only to look as far as my own dad. He was always there for me. Or to put it in today's slang, "He showed up." It didn't matter whether I had a fall from my bike or a piano recital or I was giving birth to my first child. He was always there to bandage a knee, cheer me on, or share in the most incredible joy I've ever felt in my life. He showed up.

Nate Hutchinson wants to show up, too, but he doesn't have a child of his own until an old friend leaves a posthumous request that he bring up her son.

This is no baby. Landry is a fourteen-year-old boy with a mind of his own. Landry doesn't understand why Nate would want him and he's not much interested in sticking around to find out why.

Enter Brooke Mitchell. She loves and protects her own son, Cole, fiercely—even when scandal threatens.

With Brooke and Cole there to help, Nate and Landry begin to see what they too can have, if they dare to become a family. The question is, can they do it on their own? Do they even want to try, given the fact that the two boys have become like brothers? As for Nate and Brooke—something wonderful is happening there, too…

Happy reading!

Cathy Gillen Thacker

THE MUMMY PROPOSAL

BY
CATHY GILLEN THACKER

All the characters in this book have no existence outside the imagination of the author, and have no relation whatsoever to anyone bearing the same name or names. They are not even distantly inspired by any individual known or unknown to the author, and all the incidents are pure invention.

First published in Great Britain 2011
by Mills & Boon, an imprint of Harlequin (UK) Limited,
Eton House, 18-24 Paradise Road, Richmond, Surrey TW9 1SR

© Cathy Gillen Thacker 2010

Originally published as *The Mommy Proposal*.

ISBN: 978 0 263 88917 8

23-1011

Harlequin (UK) policy is to use papers that are natural, renewable and recyclable products and made from wood grown in sustainable forests. The logging and manufacturing processes conform to the legal environmental regulations of the country of origin.

Printed and bound in Spain
by Blackprint CPI, Barcelona

Cathy Gillen Thacker is married and a mother of three. She and her husband spent eighteen years in Texas and now reside in North Carolina. Her mysteries, romantic comedies and heartwarming family stories have made numerous appearances on bestseller lists, but her best reward, she says, is knowing one of her books made someone's day a little brighter. A popular author for many years, she loves telling passionate stories with happy endings, and thinks nothing beats a good romance and a hot cup of tea! You can visit Cathy's website at www.cathygillenthacker.com for more information on her upcoming and previously published books, recipes and a list of her favorite things.

Chapter One

"I hear you work miracles," Nate Hutchinson drawled.

"Sometimes I do." Brooke Mitchell smiled and took the sexy financier's hand in hers, shaking it briefly as she stepped into his downtown Fort Worth office.

"Good." Nate looked her straight in the eye. "Because I'm in need of a home makeover—fast. The son of an old friend is coming to live with me."

Still tingling from the feel of his warm, hard palm clasped in hers, Brooke stepped back. "Temporarily or permanently?"

"If all goes according to plan, I'll adopt Landry by summer's end."

Brooke had heard the founder of Nate Hutchinson Financial Services was eligible, wealthy and generous to a fault. She hadn't known he was in the market for a family, but she supposed she shouldn't be surprised. Nate's four best buddies were all married, with kids. It made sense that as he approached his late thirties, the dark-haired, six-foot-five Texan would want to enrich his personal life, too. Brooke had just figured that a man as successful and handsome as Nate would want to do so the old-fashioned way. By finding a woman to settle down with and *then* have babies. Not that this was any of her business, she reminded herself sternly.

She turned her glance away from Nate's broad shoulders and powerful chest. "So how old is this child?" she asked in a crisp, formal tone, trying not to think how the marine-blue of Nate Hutchinson's dress shirt and striped tie deepened the hue of his eyes.

"Fourteen."

Brooke sank into a chair and pulled out a notepad and pen. She crossed her legs at the knee and continued. "What's he like?"

"I don't know." Nate circled around to sit behind his massive antique mahogany desk. He relaxed against the smooth leather of the chair. "I've never met him."

"You've invited this kid to live with you permanently and you've never laid eyes on him?" Brooke blurted before she could stop herself.

Nate flashed a charming half smile, the kind car salesmen gave when they were talking about gas mileage that was less than ideal. "It's complicated," he murmured. "But I'm sure it's going to work out fine."

Obviously, Brooke thought, calling on her own experience as a parent, Nate Hutchinson knew as little about teenage boys as he did about decorating. But that wasn't her problem. Finding a way to do the assignment and collect her commission without getting emotionally involved was. It seemed there hadn't been a child born yet in this world who did not possess the capability to steal her heart…and that went double for a kid in any kind of trouble.

The phone on his desk buzzed. Nate picked up. "Yes. Send him in. I want Ms. Mitchell to meet him." He rose and headed for the door.

Moments later, a tall, gangly teen sauntered through the portal of the executive suite. He wore jeans and a faded T-shirt he had clearly outgrown, and had peach fuzz on his face and shaggy dishwater-blond hair. His only nod toward propriety was the tender deference with which he treated the elderly white-haired woman beside him. She walked with a cane and looked so frail even a mild Texas breeze might blow her over.

Brooke could feel Nate's shock, even as he resumed the perennial smooth of someone who made his living charming people into investing with his firm. "Mrs. Walker. It's been a long time." He moved to help her into a chair. The youth assisted from the other side.

The elderly woman gratefully accepted their help. "Yes. It has."

"And this must be your great-grandson." Nate moved toward the fourteen-year-old boy, genially extending his palm. "Hello, Landry."

Hands shoved in the pockets of his jeans, Landry looked around the luxuriously appointed office, ignoring Nate entirely. Finally, with a disgruntled sigh, he cast a sideways glance at his great-grandmother. "Obviously, this isn't going to work, Gran. So…can we go now?"

"Landry, dear, I explained…" Mrs. Walker replied in a feeble tone.

Landry scowled at Nate. "I don't care how much money this dude has!" he blurted. "There's no way he's going to adopt me and be my dad!"

NATE COULDN'T BLAME the teen for being upset with the quick turn of events. He hadn't seen this coming, either.

Had it been anyone but Jessalyn Walker asking him to do this, he would have been on the phone to his lawyer, seeking another solution. But it *was* Jessalyn who was here, orphan in tow. And it had been her granddaughter Seraphina making the request, through a letter left for

Nate. A letter Jessalyn had held on to until yesterday, while she, too, tried to do what was best for all concerned.

Nate dropped his hand. "I'm very sorry about your loss," he said quietly.

"My mom died a year and a half ago." The teen glared at him, still hovering protectively next to his great-grandmother. "If you were really my mom's friend, where were you then? You should have been there."

What could Nate say to that? The kid was right. "Had I known your mother was ill, I would have been," he assured him.

Landry looked at him contemptuously.

"He's here now, Landry, ready and willing to help us— just the way your mom wanted, when the day came that I could no longer care for you." Jessalyn Walker reached out and put a comforting hand on her great-grandson's forearm. "That's all that counts."

Landry's chin quivered. "You don't have to take care of me," he declared. "I'll take care of you."

"That's not the way it's supposed to be," Jessalyn reminded him patiently, giving his arm another beseeching pat.

Landry broke away abruptly. "I don't mind. I want to do it!"

"Landry—" Jessalyn pleaded.

"If you don't want me around, fine! Go ahead and move into that retirement center!" Landry huffed. "But I'm not signing on for *this!* And none of you can make me!" He spun around and strode toward the door.

Nate took off after him, catching up with Landry before he reached the elevators. Nate had no experience with wayward teenagers, but he was pretty certain he knew what was called for here. "If you care about your great-grandmother as much as you say you do, you'll come back to that office and work things out like a man instead of running away."

Landry snorted. "Whatever." He did an about-face and marched back to the office, spine straight, attitude intact. Nate followed him.

Brooke, who had been consoling Jessalyn, gently squeezed the woman's frail hand and met Nate's gaze.

"I know you are furious at my failing health. So am I," Jessalyn Walker told her great-grandson wearily. "But my doctor is right. I need more care than I can get at home. And you can't live with me in the assisted-living home I'm moving into tomorrow. So it's either go with Nate today, and give that a try as I've asked, or enter the foster care system."

Landry's scowl deepened.

To Nate's surprise, Brooke stepped into the fray. She fixed Landry with a kind look. "I know this is none of my business, but I would advise you to go with Nate. I was in foster care as a kid. I got moved around a lot. It was…not fun."

This, Nate had not known.

Landry's eyes narrowed. "Is that the truth?"

Brooke nodded sadly. "I lost both my mom and dad when I was fourteen, but unlike you, had no relatives or old family friends to take me in." She paused, regarding the teenager with a gaze that was as matter-of-fact as it was softly maternal. "Not having any family at all to care about you is a tough way to grow up. I really wouldn't recommend it, honey."

Landry's shoulders sagged. "Can I live with you then?" he asked Brooke.

She seemed as taken aback by the request as everyone

else in the room, and exhaled ruefully. "I'm sorry, Landry, but that is not an option."

He crossed his arms in front of him. "Then I'll take foster care," he insisted.

Seeing a situation he had hoped would go smoothly rapidly deteriorate into emotional chaos was not part of Nate's plan. Determined to regain control of the moment, he caught Brooke's attention and gestured toward the door. "If you two will excuse us, I'd like to talk to Ms. Mitchell alone a moment."

Brooke didn't appear to want to go with him, but complied nevertheless. Her posture regal, she walked down the hall to the boardroom. Nate held the door, then followed her inside.

The room was elegantly appointed, with a long table and comfortable leather chairs backed by a floor-to-ceiling window overlooking the Trinity River and downtown Fort Worth. The spectacular view was nothing compared to the tall, slender woman standing in front of it.

Nate paused, taking in the glossy fall of walnut-brown hair brushing her shoulders. A sleeveless tunic showcased her shapely arms. Matching silk trousers fluidly draped her legs. But it was the inherent kindness and empathy in her golden-brown eyes he found the most captivating. It was no wonder Landry had gravitated to her. Brooke Mitchell was an intriguing mix of savvy business entrepreneur and empathetic woman. She seemed like someone who would know what to do in any situation. And right now, Nate and Landry both needed a woman like that in their lives.

She glanced out at the skyline, then turned back to him. "I understand you have a big problem," she told him with all sincerity. "I *feel* for Landry. But there my involvement ends."

Nate remained determined. "I understand you're a single mother with a thirteen-year-old boy."

A delicate blush silhouetted her high, sculpted cheeks. "How did you…?"

"Alexis McCabe mentioned it when she gave me your name and suggested you were the ideal person to help me make the mansion I just purchased a home." Nate walked over to stand next to her. He glanced out at the view, too, then back at her. "I need help getting Landry situated."

Brooke inclined her head slightly to one side. "As a single parent, you have to get used to handling these challenges by yourself."

Again Nate followed the spill of glossy hair brushing her shoulders, and couldn't help but notice her fair skin and toned body. She was one sexy lady, in the woman-in-the-office-across-the-hall kind of way. And due to the circumstances he and Landry were facing, totally off-limits. Nate needed to keep his thoughts trained on the issue at hand.

"I will handle these problems myself," he promised her, "as soon as Landry adjusts to the idea of becoming my son."

She remained silent, but gave him a look that said *Lotsa luck with that!*

Undeterred, he braced a shoulder against the glass. "In the meantime, you have a son close to Landry's age, and I have a two-bedroom cottage on the property. You and your son could stay there while the makeover of the main house takes place, under your direction. The boys could swim in the pool, play on the sport court, and you could help bring me up to speed on this whole parenting thing."

Brooke shot him a censuring glance. "You presume a lot."

Nate countered with what experience told him would be

the winning hand. "I'm also willing to pay a lot," he said bluntly. "Double your usual rate for the next two weeks, if you'll help me out here."

Silence stretched between them, as palpable as the sexual sparks he'd felt when he had first taken her hand. Brooke's services were expensive to begin with. They were talking a lot of money here. "You're serious," she said.

"As a heartbeat."

Brooke sighed and then muttered something under her breath he couldn't quite catch. "All right," she said finally, lifting a nicely manicured hand to her hair. "I'll do it on several conditions."

Nate stepped closer, inhaling the soft lilac fragrance of her perfume. "And those are?"

Her fine brow arched. "When my work at your place is done, I'm done with the whole situation."

Nate lifted his hands in surrender. "No problem."

Her pert chin angled higher. "Two, if the boys don't get along, they won't be forced to hang out together."

Nate agreed readily. "All right."

"Three. My son, Cole, is already enrolled for the summer in a prestigious academic day camp that focuses on computer skills, and he's going to go."

Nate had been involved in organized activities—mostly academic—every summer when he was a kid, too, and always enjoyed them. "That might be good for Landry, as well."

"If you can get him in, it probably would be great for him," Brooke agreed. "And four, I make no guarantee how this will all work out. Except to say that you will be pleased with how your home looks when the redecoration is complete."

Nate admired her confidence. Curious, and more than a little intrigued by the beautiful and accomplished woman in front of him, he asked, "How do you know that?" She hadn't even seen the property or heard what he had in mind.

Brooke's radiant smile lit up the room. "When it comes to my work, I never give up until the customer is completely satisfied."

Chapter Two

"Not exactly child-friendly, is it?" Brooke observed, walking through Nate Hutchinson's multimillion-dollar residence an hour later.

The ten-thousand-square-foot abode had a postmodern edge to it. Everything was black or white. Glass tables and lamps abounded, as did expensive statues and paintings. The overall impression she got was sleek, cold and sterile.

Nate shrugged. "It's an investment. I bought it as is. It can all be changed."

He glanced over at Landry and his great-grandmother. The teen was glumly inspecting the marble-floored foyer and sweeping staircase. Jessalyn was sitting wearily in the formal library, off to the left. Cane in hand, she kept a worried gaze on the boy. Probably wondering, Brooke thought, if Landry was going to be able to accept his new living arrangements.

"Obviously," Nate continued, oblivious to the concerned nature of Brooke's thoughts, "we'll set a budget that is appropriate for the scope and scale of this house." He paused, close enough now that she took in the fragrance of his soap, cologne and heady male essence. "I'm going to need it done as quickly as possible. Two weeks, at the outside."

Brooke shook off the tantalizing fragrance of leather and spice. "That's a tall order."

He eyed her with lazy assurance. "I'm not worried. You have a reputation for providing your clients with the home environments they always dreamed of having, in record time."

Brooke could not contest that. She was good at what she did. She worked hard to keep at a minimum the chaos and disarray that went along with redecorating. Usually, however, the homes were not nearly this large. A feeling of nervousness sifted through her. "It's going to require a lot of time on your part, as well," she warned.

He regarded her with maddening nonchalance. "I don't move furniture."

Famous last words, Brooke thought. No one got through a major upheaval of their personal belongings without eventually having to heft or slightly reposition *something.* It didn't matter how many professionals were hired. At the end of the day, there was always something that wasn't quite right. Something that begged the owner to reach out and touch and, in the process, claim it as his or her own. But figuring Nate wouldn't understand the need to put his own signature on the place if it were truly to become his home, she let it go for now.

Giving him the smile she reserved for her most difficult and demanding clients, she tried again. "I meant you're going to have to sit down with me—pronto—and talk about what kind of style you envision having here."

Brooke turned as she saw Landry heading up the staircase.

Nate lifted a staying hand. "It's okay. He's going to have to explore the place sometime."

Meanwhile, Brooke noted, the seventy-nine-year-old Jessalyn appeared to be drifting off to sleep.... "So when can we get together to do this?" she asked.

"How about tonight?"

If only that were possible, she mused, as anxious to get a head start on this task as he. "I have to pick up my son at summer camp."

"Bring him, too. Say around seven? We'll all have dinner. If you want, you could even move your things into the caretaker's house at that time."

Brooke had heard Nate moved fast. His indefatigable drive had turned his solo financial advising practice into a firm with six thousand top-notch certified financial planners, and a national reputation for excellence.

She gazed up at him. "I know you want to get this done," she began.

"It's important for Landry that this feel like a home instead of a museum," Nate said.

Brooke couldn't disagree with that. "But there's such a thing as moving too fast. Decorating decisions made in haste are often repented in leisure." And she had her own problems to triumph over, starting with her promise to reconfigure her priorities and bring balance back into her life.

Nate brushed off her concern with a shrug. "I'm counting on you to help me avoid that."

The doorbell rang before she could answer him.

Nate moved to get it.

A stunning ebony-haired woman in a Marc Jacobs suit strode in, cell phone and briefcase in hand. She was in her mid-thirties, of Asian-American descent.

"Brooke Mitchell, my attorney, Mai Tanous. Mai, this is Brooke Mitchell."

Mai nodded briefly in acknowledgment, then leaned toward Nate. "We need to talk."

NATE HAD AN IDEA of what Mai was going to say. He also knew she would be much more circumspect if they weren't alone. He motioned for Brooke to stay put, and regarded Mai steadily. "I presume you brought the papers?" he asked in a voice that tolerated no argument.

Mai cast an uncertain look at Brooke, as unwilling to talk business with an audience as Nate had presumed she would be. "Yes," she said politely. "I did. But—"

He held up a hand, cutting off her protest. "Then let's sign them so Jessalyn can go home. She's exhausted."

Exhaling in frustration, Mai frowned. "Are you sure you want to do this?"

He nodded. For a moment Mai seemed torn between doing her job and being his friend. Finally, she pivoted and headed for the library, where Jessalyn was seated. As Brooke and Nate entered the room, the elderly woman roused.

Mai extended a hand and introduced herself. "Mrs. Walker, are you sure you don't want to have your own attorney present?"

Jessalyn waved off the suggestion. "I trust this man every bit as much as my late granddaughter did. If Nate says he'll do right by Landry, then he will."

"I would still feel better if we slowed down a bit," Mai said. "Perhaps began the process with a simple visit."

Nate gave his attorney a quelling glance. "I told you it wasn't necessary," he stated firmly. "Now, if you have the Power of Appointment papers..."

Her posture stiff, her expression deferential, Mai opened up her briefcase, extracted the documents. "Basically, this agreement states that Landry will live with Nate now. It gives Nate the power to take him to the doctor, and to school or camp while he is in Nate's care. In the eyes of the law, however, Landry's great-grandmother, Jessalyn Walker, will remain his legal custodian until the court transfers custodianship to Nate."

"Why can't we just make Nate Landry's legal custodian now?" Jessalyn asked impatiently.

Mai regarded the elderly woman gently. "The court will need to be certain this arrangement is in the best interest of your great-grandson."

Nate noticed Brooke visibly react to that admission.

"I don't see why, since Nate has agreed to be the father that Landry needs." Jessalyn appeared upset.

Mai knelt in front of her and took her hand. Looking her in the eye, then explained, "The authorities are still going to want home studies to be done by social workers, and reports given to the court, recommending placement. But that won't happen until the petition for custodianship is filed with the court. And in fact—" the attorney gave her hand a final pat and stood, addressing all of them once again "—I would suggest that until Landry settles in a little bit and feels like this is something he wants, too, that we hold off on taking him before a judge. And instead just let him live here for a few weeks and get used to things, before we actually petition the court to begin the process to make it permanent."

Although Brooke had said nothing during this whole exchange, Nate noticed that she seemed to agree with Mai on that. Probably because she was a mother herself and understood how unhappy Landry was right now….

No one there seemed to have confidence that Nate could make the teen any happier. When it came right down to it, he wasn't certain, either. His own familial background left a lot to be desired, in that regard.

Jessalyn studied Mai with faded blue eyes. "You're worried what will happen if Landry decides he doesn't want to live here with Nate, aren't you?"

As direct as always, the lawyer nodded, her expression grim.

"Why don't I check on Landry?" Brooke interjected helpfully.

Appreciating her discretion and sensitivity, Nate shot her a grateful glance. "Good idea."

She slipped out. The mood in the room was somber as Jessalyn and Nate read and signed the legal documents Mai had drawn up. Finally, it was done. Everyone had a copy of the Power of Appointment to take with them.

"Obviously," Nate told Jessalyn, "you are welcome to call or come by at any time to see Landry. And I'll make certain he visits you at the retirement village, too."

"Thank you," Jessalyn said, her eyes moist. "And thank you for coming to our aid. Especially under the circumstances." Her words were rife with meaning only Nate understood.

Reminded of the situation that had prompted him to cut ties with Seraphina and her grandmother, Nate bent and clasped the elderly woman's frail shoulders in a brief hug. "I wish you'd come to me sooner," he murmured in her ear.

Jessalyn looked at him. "You know why I didn't," she retorted, just as quietly.

Nate did. He exhaled deeply. Before he could reply, Brooke appeared in the doorway.

"A small problem," she said with a rueful twist of her lips. "I can't find Landry anywhere."

MAI STAYED WITH a visibly upset Jessalyn Walker. Brooke and Nate split up. She covered the east half of the house, while he covered the west. Both were diligent in their search. Neither found a trace of the wayward teen.

Mute with worry, they headed out to the lagoon-style swimming pool, complete with elaborate greenery. He wasn't there. Ditto the sport court. The detached six-car garage. The only thing left was the caretaker's cottage.

"Naturally," Nate murmured, as they approached the

porch of the ranch-style domicile and spied Landry settled in front of the television inside. "He's in the last place we looked."

"And also," Brooke noted thoughtfully, "the most eclectic."

Unlike the house, Brooke observed, which had been decorated with style and cutting-edge decor in mind, the cottage was a ramshackle collection of mismatched furniture and odds and ends. It was, in short, a designer's nightmare—and a disgruntled teen's hideout.

Surprised and a little disappointed to suddenly find herself in the same situation she had endured in her youth, she pivoted toward Nate. He stepped nearer at the same time. Without warning, she was suddenly so close to him she couldn't avoid the brisk masculine fragrance of his cologne, or the effect it had on her senses. Turning to her cool professionalism, she stepped back slightly. "This is where you wanted me and my son to stay?"

Nate's brow furrowed. Obviously, he saw no problem with the arrangement, but was astute enough to realize she was momentarily disconcerted. Not just at the obvious discrepancy between this and the main house, but what the decision obviously said about his estimation of her. This was no cozy abode, or the sort of lodging suitable for a respected colleague. Rather, it was a place for a servant one didn't care much about. Worse, there was a thick layer of dust on every surface, which would play havoc with her son's asthma.

"It doesn't look like it's been cleaned in forever," Brooke stated grimly. And Nate had wanted her and her son to stay there that night!

"I apologize for that," Nate murmured, clapping a hand on the back of his neck. "I was unaware."

Typical man. Brooke sighed in displeasure. This job

hadn't even started yet and it was already a mess in practically every respect. She had half a mind to forgo the lucrative contract and walk out.

"I suggested it because it was separate from the house, and therefore private. I hadn't really thought about the condition of the place or the decor. I haven't used it in the two months I've lived here. Nor has anyone else, since I don't employ any live-in help." Nate took another look through the window. "But I see why you're less than tempted to accept. I guess for someone like you, who pays attention to the aesthetics, these accommodations could be…"

"Insulting?"

"It's not what I meant when I issued the invitation." He ran a hand through his thick black hair and looked seriously chagrined.

Brooke let him off the hook with a raised eyebrow.

Clearly not one to let a mistake of any kind go, Nate persisted with narrowed eyes, "Obviously, we'll get this place scrubbed from top to bottom, and fixed up, too. And we'll take care of that before we even start on the main house, if you do agree to move in here with your son."

Brooke had not come this far in her career to get the reputation of a diva. And if the story got out that Nate had been forced to redo her quarters before starting on his own, her competitors would have a field day. She stopped him with a glance. "It's not a problem. I've lived in worse. Foster care, remember?"

"Oh."

"I can make anyplace a home." In fact, she told herself sternly, she welcomed the challenge.

At the moment there were far more pressing problems to deal with.

Brooke cast another look at the fourteen-year-old slumped on the hideously out-of-date orange-green-and-brown-plaid sofa. "Let's go inside and talk to Landry," she murmured, touching Nate's arm.

The boy was the picture of defiance as the two adults entered the cottage.

"You can't run off like that," Nate chided, switching off the television.

Landry leaped up, hands balled at his sides. "Who are you to tell me what to do?" he demanded. "And don't go saying you're going to be my dad, because you're not!"

Nate explained about the legal papers that had been signed.

Landry fell silent. "So I'll live here," he grudgingly agreed at last. "It doesn't change the fact that you're just some guy doing a favor for my great-grandma." He stormed out of the cottage and back toward the house, leaving Brooke and Nate no choice but to follow.

In Landry's place, Brooke knew she would have been wary, too. Seeking a reason that would alleviate the orphaned child's distrust, she inquired matter-of-factly, "Why haven't you been part of Landry's life until now?"

For a moment, Nate didn't answer. Finally, he explained, "I didn't know he existed until twenty-four hours ago, when Jessalyn Walker called me. She told me Seraphina had died of cancer a year and a half ago, and that Landry had been living with her ever since. Jessalyn said at first it was all right. He was clearly grieving the loss, as was she, but they were a team. Then, in the last month or so, as her health began to fail and she had to sell her home and arrange to move into the assisted-living facility, he became really angry about the hand fate had dealt him."

Understandably so, Brooke mused.

"He did his best to care for her, apparently, and convince her she didn't need nurses looking after her, when she had him," Nate related. "But she knew Landry deserved a better life. So she took a letter that Seraphina had left behind, for a worst-case scenario, and had it messengered to me."

And the combination of phone call and letter had worked to get Nate involved.

"What did the letter say?" Brooke asked, telling herself that her curiosity had nothing to do with her interest in Nate the man and his previous relationship with Landry's mother, and everything to do with trying to create a home decor that worked for both Nate and his charge. There might be clues in that note about what his mother thought her son would one day want and need....

Nate reached into the pocket of his suit jacket. Wordlessly, he handed over a piece of cream-colored stationery. Brooke opened it and read:

Dear Nate,
Landry needs a man he can look up to in his life. I know I have no right to ask you this after the way our engagement ended, but please put the past aside and be the family to my son that my grandmother Jessalyn and I can no longer be. And if you can't do that, I trust you to find someone who can give Landry all the care and attention he is going to need in the years ahead.
I never stopped loving you.
Seraphina.

Finished, Brooke handed the letter back. It was obvious Seraphina had really looked up to Nate, despite whatever had transpired to break them up. "Why didn't she ask you to do this before she died?"

Nate's tone grew turbulent. "Probably because she didn't

know how I'd feel or what I'd do. When she knew me, I was all-career, all the time."

"And yet she trusted you either to be the father Landry needed or to find one for him."

"What can I say?" The emotion in Nate's eyes dissipated and he flashed a charming grin. "I'm a trustworthy guy."

What wasn't he telling her? Brooke wondered. Did it have anything to do with the reason Nate and Seraphina had stopped communicating and made little or no effort to remain friends after their breakup?

Brooke studied Nate, the mother in her coming to the fore. "Are you sure you want to take this on?" Landry had already weathered a lot of loss. Nate had no experience with children, and gallantry, no matter how well intentioned, took a potential parent only so far.

He nodded, his blue eyes serious. "In the end Seraphina and I may not have been right for each other, but I loved her, too, and always will. And I know I can—and will—love her son."

"YOU'VE GOT TO BE kidding me!" Cole said, when Brooke picked him up at day camp several hours later. He regarded her with all the disdain a thirteen-year-old boy could muster. "What about the promise you made to me about not taking on any more ridiculously demanding clients and 'restoring balance' to our life?"

Brooke had meant it at the time. She still did. "I had to take this job," she explained.

She eased away from the carpool line and pulled out onto the street. Her minivan picked up speed as she drove. "Because the circumstances were extenuating—and Alexis McCabe asked me to do it, as a special favor. And I owe her...you know that." Brooke let out a beleaguered sigh.

"Not only was she one of my very first customers, after your dad died. She helped me get my business off the ground, with tons of referrals." To the point Brooke was now doing only big projects, with unlimited budgets.

"I liked it better when your clients weren't so rich they felt they could ask you to do anything and you'd have to say yes."

So had Brooke, in the sense that she hadn't felt so pressured. That the more prestigious jobs brought better pay... well, she was happy with that. "I know. And if my last client hadn't canceled the job abruptly—"

"When you refused to fly to Paris to look at fabric."

Brooke nodded. That client had been outrageously demanding—and unreasonable. "I guess it all worked out for the best. If I'd abided by his wishes, I wouldn't have unexpectedly had two weeks open...or been able to take this job with Nate Hutchinson." She couldn't help smiling. *Now I'm going to get paid double my usual rate for two weeks!*

"This Hutchinson guy...he's an important dude?"

Brooke glanced at her son. As usual, Cole looked relaxed and content after a day spent alternately learning cool stuff and playing in the summer sunshine. He was dressed in a yellow camp T-shirt with a computer emblazoned on the front, khaki cargo shorts and sneakers. That day's athletic activity had been swimming, so his blond hair was wet and smelled of chlorine.

"One of the most high-profile businessmen in Fort Worth," she confirmed.

"And he knows a lot about money."

"Apparently so, judging by the success of his financial services company."

Cole sighed. "Yeah, well...I still don't want to live in some guy's house!"

Nor did Brooke, to tell the truth. But every time she remembered the look on Landry's face, she thought about her own experiences in foster care—what it had felt like to get shunted around to places you didn't know, with people you'd never met—and her heart went out to him. She knew she could help him adjust. And if doing so eventually repaid the universe's kindness to her…

"It's actually a caretaker's cottage, and it's a rush job. The only way I'll get it done in the time allotted is if I'm at the Hutchinson estate day and night for the next two weeks. And if I'm there till all hours and you're at our place…"

Cole grabbed the half-finished sport drink from his backpack and unscrewed the top. His golden-brown eyes were wiser than his years. "We'll never see each other."

"Right." Brooke turned onto the entrance ramp that would take them to the freeway. "I know you're at camp all day. But I still like hanging around with you during the evenings, even when I have to spend part of that time working."

Cole ripped open the wrapper on an energy bar. "If I'm a good sport about this, you're going to owe me."

Brooke had no problem putting the carrot ahead of the stick. Incentives were a great way to motivate people into going the extra mile. She smiled at her boyishly handsome son. "What would you like?"

Cole beamed and bartered resolutely, "A whole day at the Six Flags amusement park in Arlington! We're there when the park opens and we stay until we see the fireworks. Deal?"

Brooke consented with a nod, glad to have come to some accord. "Deal. But it's going to have to wait until I finish the job," she cautioned.

He wiped the oatmeal crumbs off his mouth with the

back of his hand. "Or sooner, if you get a day off before then."

Brooke wouldn't count on that. She had just met the man, but... "Mr. Hutchinson can be quite the slave driver."

"You can sweet-talk him into letting you have a day off next weekend. You can sweet-talk anybody, Mom."

Brooke knew that was true. But only to a point. "And there is one more thing," she added, turning into the neighborhood of palatial estates Fort Worth's wealthiest citizens called home.

"Uh-oh," Cole said. "I know that look...."

Brooke tried to focus on the positive. "Mr. Hutchinson has a boy your age who is just now coming to live with him. Landry's mom died a year and a half ago, so he's having a hard time." Briefly, she explained what had transpired.

Cole fell silent, no doubt thinking about the death of his own father two years before, and the grief he had endured.

Finally, he asked, "Was Landry's great-grandmother nice when you met her?"

"Very nice. She's just too old and too ill to care for him." Brooke turned into the drive. She keyed in the pass code that Nate had given her before she left. The electric gates opened.

"Wow," Cole murmured, sitting up in his seat. "This is rich!"

At the end of the driveway, near the huge detached garage, Landry was kicking a landscaping stone across the pavement. Scowling, he barely looked up as she parked her minivan.

Cole's compassionate expression faded, and wariness kicked in. "Is that the kid?" he asked.

Brooke nodded.

Her son tensed. "He doesn't look friendly at all."

It didn't matter. The success of this particular job meant the kids had to develop a rapport. So for all their sakes, she would use every one of the skills she possessed to make sure they did.

Chapter Three

Landry grumbled the moment he laid eyes on the supper selections. "There are dead fish on this pizza."

Brooke knew it was a mistake to have Landry's first meal with Nate in the formal dining room. The black lacquer table seated fifty. But there was no other place to eat inside the house, since the equally enormous kitchen was set up like a fancy hotel cook space, with stainless-steel counters and massive state-of-the-art appliances. So she had ignored her own instincts—which were to dine at one of the wrought-iron tables outside on the terrace—and gone along with Nate's suggestion.

Nate looked momentarily taken aback by Landry's disdain. "I had them put anchovies on only one of the pies."

Landry stared at the dinner laid out for them, thanks to the local upscale pizza-delivery service. "That purple stuff looks gross, too."

Nate glanced down at the colorful assortment of veggies topping another crust. "That's grilled eggplant. And if you don't like it, you could remove it and just eat the rest of the vegetables."

That suggestion was met with mute resistance.

"Maybe you could try the Hawaiian pizza," Brooke suggested kindly.

Landry scowled. "Who puts pineapple and ham on top of cheese and tomato sauce?"

"Actually, you'd be surprised. It's pretty good." Cole held out his plate. "I'll have some," he said.

Nate cheerfully handed over a generous slice.

"You might like it," Brooke told Landry.

The boy stared glumly at the last option—a pale pizza with spinach and garlic—then looked back at Brooke. His great-grandmother had only been gone an hour, she thought. Already Landry was near meltdown. Her heart went out to him. Leaving Jessalyn would have been tough under any circumstances. Going to a place he didn't know, to be with an old family friend he had never met...

She touched his arm lightly and offered a comforting smile. Landry gazed into her eyes, then wordlessly held out his plate. "My mom used to look at me like that, when she wanted me to do something I didn't want to do," he muttered beneath his breath.

Which was as close as they were going to get to verbal capitulation, Brooke thought, as she served him a slice of Hawaiian pizza. "You have to eat," she said, using every ounce of motherly persuasion in her arsenal. "Otherwise, you're only going to feel worse."

Landry exhaled, bent his head over his plate, took a bite. Then another...and another.

Nate asked Cole how summer camp was going. Smiling, he launched into an account of everything he had done in the first two weeks. Brooke's pride in her son's outgoing nature and accomplished social skills was tempered by her concern for Landry. The orphaned child was so out of his depth here. Worse, she wasn't sure Nate had the tools to reach him.

"Perhaps your attorney had a point," she said half an hour later, when the two boys had gone outside to hit some tennis balls around the sport court behind the swimming pool. She cleared the table while Nate put the leftover pizza away. "Maybe you should slow this process down a bit, have Landry get to know you better first."

"And put him where? Jessalyn's heart is failing. She's moving into a retirement village with round-the-clock nursing care tomorrow."

"She can't put it off even a short while or move in here with him temporarily?"

"I've already suggested both. It is Jessalyn's opinion that Landry won't bond with me or anyone else unless there's no other option. She does think that he'll enjoy academic camp. Apparently, he's been extremely bored since school let out for the summer, and he's as interested in computers and technology as Cole is." Nate paused. "So I'll work on getting that set up first thing tomorrow. In the meantime, I have to figure out what to do about the sleeping arrangements tonight."

"What do you mean?" Brooke asked.

"Initially, I thought I would just put Landry in one of the guest rooms, and have you and Cole bunk in the caretaker's cottage. Now I'm thinking it might be better to have you all stay in the main house this evening."

"Or we could simply go home and come back tomorrow," she offered hopefully.

Nate's glance narrowed. "I don't think Landry would like that."

She sighed. "Probably not."

Nate stepped closer.

She noticed the evening beard darkening his jaw. It lent a rugged masculinity to his already handsome features. Irritated to find herself attracted to him—again—she stepped back. She had a job to do here. One that did not involve lusting after the boss...

Oblivious to the desirous nature of her thoughts, Nate looked into Brooke's eyes. "Landry's bonding with you."

She felt drawn to him, too. Landry needed a mom in his life again. So much so that he had immediately latched onto her.

But that was no solution, Brooke realized sadly.

She fought getting any more emotionally involved in a situation that was not hers to fix. She was trying to bring *balance* to her life, not more conflict. "He needs to bond with you, Nate."

"And he will...over time," Nate concurred calmly.

A little irked to see him treating this like just another life challenge, when it was so much more than that, Brooke murmured, "Never met a target you couldn't charm?"

His persuasive smile faded, and with an understanding that seemed to go soul-deep, he murmured, "I never wanted to be in a situation where I had no family."

But here he was, Brooke thought, unmarried and childless—until today, anyway.

"And I'm certain Landry doesn't want to be in that situation, either." Nate paused, before finishing resolutely, "When he realizes we can help each other, he'll come around."

Brooke hoped so. Otherwise, all four of them were in for a bumpy ride.

"Psssst, Mom! Are you still awake?"

Her heart jumping at the urgency of the whisper, Brooke sat up in bed. "Cole?"

The guest room door eased open. Seconds later, Cole and Landry tiptoed in. Both were barefoot, clad in cotton pajama pants and T-shirts. Cole's were stylish and vibrant: Landry's were faded and on the verge of being too small.

Promising herself she would get Nate to take care of the clothes issue for Landry as soon as possible, Brooke turned on the bedside lamp. "Why aren't you two asleep?"

Cole perched on the foot of her bed, then signaled for Landry to do the same. The boy came around to the other side.

It seemed being in the same boat had forged a bond between the two, Brooke noted. Realizing a first tentative step toward Landry's future had been made, she smiled. Maybe Nate was smarter about all this than she had realized....

"Because the place is too big and too quiet." Hands clenched nervously, Landry sat down, too.

"It feels like we're in a hotel—only we're the only ones here," Cole acknowledged with a comically exaggerated shiver. "Which is kind of spooky if you think about it too much."

Ten thousand square feet of space *was* overwhelming, Brooke agreed. Especially the way the residence was decorated now, with a postmodern edge and minimal furnishings. The only television was in the master bedroom, where Nate was sleeping, so she couldn't even offer that as a distraction.

"You boys have a big day tomorrow." Both would be at summer camp all day. "I've got a lot on my schedule, too."

"Can we hang out here for a while?" Cole asked.

Landry's stomach grumbled loudly.

Suddenly, the mom in her kicked in, and Brooke knew what was really keeping them awake. "You guys wait here," she told them. "I'll be right back."

NATE HAD JUST CLIMBED into bed when he heard the soft sound of footsteps in the hallway.

He sat up, listening. It wasn't his imagination. That last creak had been the back stairs! He clamped down on an oath. Certain Landry was running away again, Nate flung back the covers and padded soundlessly down the hall, in the direction of the escape route.

But it wasn't Landry he found standing in the bright light of the kitchen—it was Brooke.

Clad in a snug-fitting tank top and yoga pants, her brown hair tousled, she was standing at one of the two big stainless steel refrigerators, staring thoughtfully at the contents.

"I know," Nate said. "I've got a little bit of everything in there."

She shot him a look over her shoulder, as at ease in his home as he wanted her to be. "And here I didn't imagine you could cook," she drawled.

"I don't. But I found out most of the women I've dated do, so it makes everyone happy if the fridge is well-stocked."

Brooke's smile faded. "Right," she murmured.

The word had a wealth of undercurrents. "Meaning?" Nate prodded.

Her lips curved upward even as the light faded from her eyes. She said in a low, cordial tone, "You have a reputation for making the women in your life very happy, while they are in your orbit."

Nate certainly tried. What point was there in spending time with someone unless it was a pleasurable experience? That didn't mean, however, that he pretended something was going to work long term when it clearly wouldn't.

"I don't fall in love easily." Although not for lack of trying. He wanted to be married and have a family.

She studied him as if trying to decide whether or not he was the womanizer some made him out to be, then brought out a bowl of fresh fruit, a loaf of artisan bread and a block of sharp cheddar. "Have you ever been in love?"

Nate handed over the serving board and bread slicer. "Once, with Landry's mother."

Brooke set to work preparing a snack, with the skill of a mom who spent a lot of time in the kitchen. "What happened to break you up? Or shouldn't I ask?"

Normally, Nate followed the gentleman's rule and did not talk about his previous relationships with women. For some reason, this was different. He wanted Brooke to understand. "I was working really long hours, getting my company off the ground," he admitted, moving restlessly about the sleek, utilitarian kitchen. "Seraphina was pretty involved in planning our wedding, and she had an old friend living in her building. Miles Lawrence was trying to make it as a stand-up comedian, and she went to as many of his appearances as she could. I didn't worry about the amount of time they spent together. As it turns out, I should have," Nate reflected ruefully. "She broke off our engagement to run away with him."

"And had a child," Brooke interjected, perceptive as ever.

Reluctantly, Nate met her eyes. "Some eight months later."

Her hand froze in midmotion. She stared at him, already doing the math. "Is it possible that Landry is yours?"

Nate had been wondering the same thing. All he could go on was what he knew for sure. "The birth certificate lists Miles Lawrence as Landry's father."

She went back to slicing up fruit and arranging it on a serving platter. "What about this Miles? Where is he?"

Nate lounged against the counter and watched the competent motions of her dainty hands. "Jessalyn told me yesterday that he left Seraphina before the baby was

born. Miles wanted to focus on building an act that re-
volved around being a single guy, one always in love with
a woman he could never hope to get."

Brooke looked horrified. "Don't tell me the man insisted
he had to be chasing skirts to get material...."

Nate folded his arms across his chest, sharing her disdain. "Apparently so. Anyway, Seraphina was still in love
with him and hoped he would come around and change his
mind about marrying her and building a family together,
if she gave him a little time. That's what Jessalyn told me.
But they never had a chance to find out. He died in a plane
crash when Landry was just two months old."

Brooke offered a commiserating glance. "So Landry
never knew him."

Nate shook his head. "According to Jessalyn, all he has
are a few old photographs and stories from his mom."

Brooke's smooth brow furrowed. "So what are you
going to do?"

What could he do? "Raise him as mine."

"Without finding out?" Once again, Brooke looked
shocked.

She was beginning to sound like his attorney. "There's
no point in it. I've already agreed to adopt Landry and
bring him up as my son." What counted, Nate knew, was
the commitment made, and kept. Love would follow, over
time. At least he hoped that would be the case. Thus far,
Landry didn't seem to have his heart open to anything
except rebellion.

The tromp of youthful footsteps sounded on the back
stairs. Seconds later, Landry and Cole came barreling into
the kitchen. Cole nodded at Nate, then turned back to his
mom. "Where have you been?" he demanded.

"We thought maybe you got lost," Landry added, ignoring Nate altogether and looking at Brooke with concern.

Abruptly, the teenager swung around toward Nate, suspicious as ever. "How come you're up?" he demanded.

Nate straightened. He had to find a way to get Landry to respect him. The first step was telling it like it was, in situations like this. "I heard something and thought you might be taking off again," he informed him matter-of-factly.

An inscrutable light came into Landry's eyes. It was followed swiftly by a smirk. "And so what? You were going to stop me?"

Nate nodded with the quiet authority he knew Landry needed. "That's my job now."

When Landry sullenly turned away, Nate knew he'd gotten his point across.

"It's going to take time for Landry to adjust," Brooke told Nate, after the boys had taken their snacks and headed upstairs.

How long? Nate wondered, aware that Landry was already giving Brooke a much easier time.

But then again, Nate realized, Brooke wasn't the adult legally aiding Landry's great-grandmother in keeping Landry here against his wishes....

Brooke patted his arm before heading back upstairs, too. "In the meantime you've got to be patient and follow the plan you've set out and give him plenty of positive things to do."

NATE KNEW BROOKE WAS right. So first thing the following morning, he took Landry to the academic camp where Cole was enrolled in the summer program. He and Landry talked to the director, took the tour. As they headed back to her office, the teen shrugged and muttered, "I guess it'll be okay. Can I be in the same group as Cole?"

The director nodded.

Nate filled out the paperwork, wrote a sizable check and said goodbye to Landry. Then he headed for downtown Fort Worth, and the weekly meeting with his four business partners at One Trinity River Place.

Knowing the four guys would have invaluable advice to offer, since they were all experienced parents, Nate filled the group in on everything that had happened the last few days, starting with Jessalyn's phone call and the letter from her late granddaughter, Seraphina.

"Time helps," Travis Carson said, with the expertise of a widower who had shepherded his own two daughters through the demise of their mother.

"In the meantime...I have to agree with your lawyer," Grady McCabe told Nate seriously. "You are jumping the gun a bit, deciding to adopt Landry before the two of you have had a chance to develop any real rapport. The promise may not ring true to him."

Nate respected Grady's inherent ability to look at the big picture. Not just in the skyscrapers and other mixed-use development projects they built, but in their personal lives, too.

Dan Kingsland added matter-of-factly, "I know you've already hired Brooke Mitchell...."

Nodding, Nate was glad he'd had the foresight to bring her on board. She was the one ray of sunshine in his chaotic life right now.

"But redecorating your house just highlights the fact you're going to have to make a lot of changes to take Landry in," Dan continued. "I can't say how he would respond to that, since I've never met him, but I know my three kids would interpret it to mean they're a burden."

Jack Gaines added, "The faster change occurs, the harder it is to accept."

Nate knew Jack and his daughter had just weathered

a lot of upheaval due to a hasty wedding in their family. But that had worked out okay in the end, too. "I have faith Brooke Mitchell will be able to pull this off," he told his friends.

"The home makeover, sure," Grady said. "Everyone knows Brooke can work miracles in that regard. That's why her services are in such high demand."

"But she's not going to be there two weeks from now when the task is finished," Dan cautioned.

"At that point," Travis interjected, "you have got to be prepared to parent solo. And the rest of us know from experience that is one of the hardest things to do."

But it could be done, Nate thought, as the meeting concluded and he headed home to confer with Brooke over the lunch hour. All he needed were a few more tips and parental insights from her to get Landry moving in the right direction. After that happened, Nate was confident that the tension in his household would fade.

When he drove in the front gates, he expected to see the cleaning van on its way out, not furniture dotting the lawn. Nor a Cadillac next to Brooke's van, with a faculty parking sticker for a local university prominently displayed. Curious, Nate walked across the lawn, hearing the voices as he rounded the house.

"You gave me no choice," the bearded, white-haired man said. "You've been ducking my calls."

"I had hoped," Brooke said archly, "that would be enough for you to *get the message*."

The elderly man countered, "You and Cole have to be at the publication party for Seamus's book."

Wary of intruding, but not about to leave Brooke to fend for herself if help was needed, Nate reluctantly stayed where he was and continued listening in.

"If you and Cole don't show up, people will start asking questions."

"And we wouldn't want that, would we?" Brooke's voice rang with contempt. "We wouldn't want anything to reflect poorly on the university!"

"We were protecting you and Cole."

"While turning a blind eye? If you had wanted to help, you should have let me know what was going on, long before that night."

"Brooke…" The gentleman held out a hand in entreaty.

She glared. "You have to leave."

He pushed a book and what looked to be some sort of engraved invitation into her hands. "Not before you agree to attend the party."

Her expression distraught, Brooke backed away.

Enough was enough. Nate walked briskly around the landscaped swimming pool toward the caretaker's cottage. He extended a hand toward the bearded man. "Nate Hutchinson. And you're…?"

"Professor Phineas Rylander, from the university where Brooke's husband taught. I was just inviting her to a pre-publication party that the English department is giving for her late husband, Seamus. It's his last work and we are very happy to be able to promote his collection of poetry. Naturally, we want Brooke and her son to attend."

Brooke pressed her fingertips to her temple. "I don't think it's going to be possible."

Professor Rylander refused to give up. "I beg you to reconsider."

Nate clapped a hand on his shoulder. "Thanks for stopping by."

"I—" the man began.

"I'll walk you to your Cadillac."

Reluctantly, the professor assented. Nate escorted him out, waited until he drove away, then returned to Brooke. She was sitting on one of the half-dozen pieces of mismatched furniture that had been moved to the lawn outside the cottage. She had the book and the invitation in her hands, and was staring down at the photo on the jacket cover.

Nate followed the direction of her gaze.

Seamus Mitchell had been handsome and distinguished. Yet Brooke was regarding the photo with utter loathing and contempt. Not exactly the reaction Nate would have expected. "Are you okay?"

She rose with quiet dignity. "No, I'm not," she said frankly. "And you know why?" Bitterness underscored her every syllable. "Because I know what it feels like to be betrayed by a loved one, too!"

Chapter Four

Brooke hadn't meant to blurt that out. But now that she had, she found she needed to unburden herself to someone who knew what it was like to be on the receiving end of such betrayal. Carefully, she set the book and the invitation on the chair she had been sitting on. "My husband didn't just die of a heart attack." That scenario would have been so much simpler to deal with. "He was in another woman's bed at the time."

Nate responded with an oath that perfectly summed up Brooke's feelings on the matter. Appreciating his empathy, she swallowed around the tight knot of emotion in her throat. She threaded both hands through her hair and continued with as much grace as she could muster. "The university didn't want a scandal. And there would have been one had word about what really happened gotten out, since Iris Lomax was Seamus's graduate assistant." Brooke exhaled deeply. "So the head of the English department, Professor Rylander, told everyone—including me—that he and Seamus had been out jogging when Seamus had the coronary." Her son still thought that was what had happened….

Nate gave her a look that said, *Not cool*. He reached over to squeeze her hand. "How did you find out that wasn't the case?"

In the worst possible way. Brooke lifted her gaze to his. "The nurse in the E.R. had no idea there was a mistress involved. She thought what the paramedics on the scene had initially been led to believe—that Seamus had been having sex with *me* at the time of his coronary. She had questions about Seamus's medical history, including a very mild heart attack the previous year that I knew nothing about." Brooke added with self-effacing honesty, "I have to say the way I reacted was not one of my finer moments." She was still embarrassed about how she had completely lost it.

Nate kept listening, his eyes kind.

Needing him to understand, as well as needing to unburden herself, Brooke confessed, "I had come to terms with the fact that my husband flirted with women the way some people breathe. I just thought it ended there." Her former naivete still hurt and embarrassed her. "Finding out it hadn't, and that Seamus had been taking some performance-enhancing drugs to keep up with all his extramarital activity—despite the known risks to someone who had already suffered a mild heart attack—was pretty devastating." She had been angry at her husband for his recklessness and his infidelity, and furious with herself for being such a fool.

"Does Cole know any of this?" Nate asked softly.

Relief softened the set of Brooke's shoulders, worked its way down her spine. "Heavens, no," she muttered emotionally. "He still thinks his oh-so-charming father walked on water." Despite the fact that Seamus had barely known Cole existed, except on the few occasions when the Irish poet had trotted him out, to show him off and enhance Seamus's own ego. "Which is why I don't want to take Cole to the book party."

Nate's eyes narrowed. "You're afraid someone will say something," he guessed.

"Although many faculty members remain in the dark about the circumstances surrounding Seamus's death, I have since come to realize some knew about his philandering." She took a deep breath. "Some of them thought I knew and was turning a blind eye, to keep the marriage intact. Others actively covered for him when he was out carousing, and helped him keep his infidelity from me."

"So if any of them were to look at you sympathetically..." Nate guessed where this was going.

Brooke nodded. "Or just react in a way that would stir questions in Cole's mind, it could be a problem. I worked very hard during the years of our marriage to protect Cole from anything unpleasant. Right now, he's secure in his father's love and the memories he has of our times together as family. He doesn't realize that anything was amiss." She crossed her arms self-consciously. "And I don't want to do anything that would take away from that. Because there were parts of our lives together that were very good." *Times when Seamus had really poured on the Irish charm.* "And that's all I want to dwell on. So going back to the English department, where Seamus and I first met..."

Once again Nate looked shocked. "You were his student, too?" he asked in surprise.

"I took one of his classes when I was a senior," Brooke admitted, with no small amount of cynicism. Looking back, she could see how gullible, how ripe for the picking she had been. But at the time, their age difference and Seamus's history as a tortured artist, and a known womanizer with a penchant for getting involved with female students, hadn't mattered. With effort, Brooke found her voice. "He was twenty years older than me, and when the writing was going well—as it was at the time—he was very sweet and kind and funny and loving." That was all she had seen. All she had needed to see.

"He made you happy."

Not ashamed to admit it, Brooke nodded. "When he asked me to marry him and give him a child, I was thrilled. I'd finally have a family again, and so would he." Maybe she'd been blind, but her first years as a devoted wife and mother had been one of the happiest times of her life. "We had Cole right away. Seamus wrote a few new poems and continued teaching. And I became consumed with building a part-time business on the side, and being a mom."

"And later?"

"We still had good times. But Seamus was under a lot of pressure. In academia, what they say about publish or perish is very true. The powers that be were on him to produce another book of poetry the university could promote." She swallowed uncomfortably. "Seamus didn't think it was that simple. He wanted to wait to be inspired, but that wasn't an option if he wanted to keep his standing in the department. So eventually he did what was expected." Brooke tried not to dwell on the fact that Seamus's mistress had no doubt supplied the muse for the latest collection of love poetry, just as Brooke had allegedly inspired his earlier work.

She sighed and went on. "He had just submitted *Love Notes from the Soul* to his previous publisher, The Poet's Press, and was waiting to hear back about whether or not they were going to buy it, when he died. Eventually, they decided they wanted to publish it posthumously, since it was his last work." Even though it wasn't his best work. Far from it, actually.

Nate studied her, as if sensing there was more. "So what are you going to do?" he asked finally.

Brooke put away her lingering feelings of anger and

resentment. "I'm not sure. The university has notified all the newspapers in the state that the book is coming out, and they're trying to get it reviewed. Since Seamus isn't here, they'd like me to speak with the press and help promote it."

"But you don't want to," Nate noted, perceptively.

She picked up the invitation and advance copy of her late husband's book and held them at her side. "Every instinct I have tells me it would be a mistake, especially since my feelings on the matter are so complicated. So I'm going to sidestep that minefield and let the university handle it. In the meantime—" she put her personal angst aside and got back to the business at hand "—I'd like to show you what I've done with the guesthouse."

"THIS IS ABSOLUTELY AMAZING," Nate murmured several minutes later, after he had completed the tour of the caretaker's cottage. The mismatched furniture had been covered with soft blue denim slipcovers, and colorful braid rugs adorned the newly polished wide-plank pine floors. Art was on the walls. Blue-and-white paisley draperies dressed up the plantation shutters on the windows. The old appliances in the kitchen sparkled, and a round table for four had been brought in and set with dishes that were as pretty and useful as everything else in the home.

Nate cast another glance at the cotton quilts on the beds, the fresh towels, rugs and shower curtain in the lone bathroom. It was like a guesthouse out of a magazine, with all the comforts one could possibly desire. "How did you make it so livable so fast?"

"Well, as you can see, I had everything moved onto the lawn, then had the cleaning service do a thorough scrubbing of the space. I put half the furniture back, keeping the pieces that were in the best shape and leaving the others outside. Which brings me to my next question." She walked out to the yard and gestured at the odds and ends. "Do you want to put these things into storage or give them to an auction house for resale, along with everything you won't be using?"

"Auction everything." The money from the sale would go a long way toward funding the makeover.

Brooke made a note on her clipboard. "You said you wanted to get away from the black-and-white color scheme."

"Right." Nate sauntered back into the cottage and gestured toward the inviting decor. "I want the main house to look as comfortable as this." Like the cozy, welcoming homes all his married friends had. A place where he could come home and put his feet up.

Brooke tapped the pen against her chin. "That's a pretty big undertaking. We're talking about furnishings for ten thousand square feet of space. And we'll have to come up with a new color scheme."

Nate felt his eyes begin to glaze over. That always happened when the discussion turned to decorating. "Whatever you decide is fine with me."

She looked at him, clearly unconvinced.

He lifted both palms in surrender. "I'm not kidding—I like your taste. You understand a lot about boys and what they need. Speaking of which…" He took a deep breath and plunged on. "I'm planning to take Landry to get a haircut this evening after camp. And then to buy the clothes he needs. Any chance you and Cole might want to join us?"

Brooke hesitated.

Nate knew he was pushing it, dragging her further into this situation. But he had no choice. Edging closer still, he threw himself on her mercy. "I know nothing about any of this. And Landry can tell. You, on the other hand, are Supermom."

She raked her teeth across her lower lip. "I don't know about that."

"I do," he said. "I could use your help. Please don't make me beg...."

As their eyes locked, Nate sensed a wall going up between them. "I meant what I said yesterday. You're going to have to learn to do this on your own eventually," Brooke stated, sizing him up with golden-brown eyes.

"*Eventually* being the key word," he agreed.

After another moment, she finally relented, as he had hoped she would.

It was Landry Nate had trouble convincing.

"No way!" the teen said when he and Cole got home from camp, and they were told the plan. "I'm not getting a haircut, and I don't want or need any new clothes."

"Why do I have to go?" Cole chimed in.

"Because you need a haircut and a new pair of shoes," Brooke told him firmly.

Cole apparently knew that tone, Nate noted. Both boys sighed in resignation and tromped back out toward the driveway, muttering under their breaths the entire way.

"Nicely done," Nate said, falling into step beside Brooke.

Her expression as resigned as her son's, she murmured back, "Don't congratulate either of us until we complete our tasks."

Nate wasn't sure what she meant. He found out twenty minutes later, when they entered the unisex hair salon. Brooke went over with Cole to talk to the stylist taking walk-in appointments, and then sat down to read a magazine.

Landry glared at Nate, cutting off any attempt on his

part to do the same. "If I have to do this, I'm doing it my way," he growled as another available stylist walked toward them.

Figuring anything would be an improvement if it got the hair out of the boy's eyes, Nate nodded and gave him free rein. "I've got a call to make. I'll be right outside."

He stepped out into the mall. When he came back twenty minutes later, Cole was finished. His hair was cut in traditional adolescent-boy layers. He looked preppy and well-groomed. Brooke seemed pleased.

Landry was finished, too.

"You don't like it, do you?" he challenged, after Nate had paid the cashier.

But Brooke's son did. "You look like a punk rocker," Cole observed admiringly.

Which, Nate figured, Landry had done to tick him off.

Aware that Landry was waiting for him to lose his cool, Nate glanced at the new cut. The hair on top of Landry's head was short, spiky and stood straight up. The rest was thinned and layered, and fell almost to his shoulders. "Looks trendy," Nate said, and left it at that.

The teen scowled. "You can't like it," he insisted.

Which meant, Nate thought, *Landry* didn't like it.

Nate shrugged. "Your hair, your choice."

The boy's eyes narrowed. All rebellious teenager again, he pointed out, "You didn't say that when you were making me *get* my hair cut."

"My bad," Nate admitted, realizing too late he shouldn't have forced the issue.

Landry continued to glare at him. Finally, realizing Nate was sincere in his reversal, he scowled and said nothing more.

Brooke glanced at Nate as the boys walked on ahead.

The empathy in her eyes made him feel better. Although he still didn't know what he was doing in terms of being the dad Landry seemed to want and need.

The two teens paused in front of a popular clothing store known for its appeal to teenagers.

As they stood there, Nate noticed the longing on Landry's face. It had obviously been months since anyone had bought clothes for him, and Jessalyn would probably not have known to come here. "This okay with you?" Nate asked.

Landry's expression transformed. He looked at the cargo-shorts and T-shirt-clad model in the window with exaggerated disdain. "Sure," he drawled sarcastically, "why not? If you're going to torture me, why not torture me all the way?"

"Enthusiasm," Nate murmured, resisting the urge to clap an affectionate hand on the lad's shoulder. "Just what I want to see." Stuffing fingers in his pockets, he followed Landry inside. Brooke and Cole sauntered in after them. The boys headed straight for the racks of T-shirts.

An hour later, they walked out with enough clothing to see Landry through the rest of the summer.

Next stop was the shoe store, where Landry and Cole both got new athletic shoes and sandals.

Hamburgers, shakes and fries followed. It was nine o'clock before they returned to Nate's place.

"We're sleeping in the caretaker's cottage tonight," Brooke told Cole, when he got out of Nate's Jaguar.

"Then I want to sleep there, too," Landry said.

Brooke looked at a loss.

Nate figured it was one battle best not fought that evening. Tabling his own disappointment, he said, "If it's okay with you, it's okay with me." His primary concern was that Landry be safe.

Brooke hesitated. It was clear she felt like a traitor to what Nate was trying to do, but also knew the dynamics of the situation. She turned and put a hand on each teen's shoulder. "Then let's go, guys."

FOR THE NEXT HOUR, Nate roamed the mansion, trying to envision how it would appear when Brooke was finished with the makeover.

The more he looked around, the more it seemed he had given her an impossible task.

The rooms were all too large. There were too many of them. Even without the contemporary black and white furnishings, it was too big and cold and sterile.

No wonder Cole and Landry had eagerly gone off with Brooke to the now-cozy caretaker's cottage.

Given the choice, Nate would have preferred the smaller abode, too.

And no wonder Landry preferred being with Brooke over him. Spending time with her probably reminded him of home.

Ironically, Cole didn't seem to mind spending time with him, Nate thought as he changed clothes and went down to the pool for a swim. In fact, Brooke's son seemed eager to get acquainted with him. It was only his son-to-be, Nate thought as he swam lap after lap, who couldn't have cared less if they developed a rapport.

And that could spell trouble in the future, he realized, as he climbed from the pool, his workout ended.

Just then the cottage door opened and Brooke crossed the lawn. Nate ran a towel over his face and hair, then draped it around his waist.

Brooke had changed out of her business clothes into a figure-hugging T-shirt, running shorts and flip-flops. She'd swept her hair into a silky knot on the back of her head. She looked pretty and at ease in that mom-next-door way.

"Landry and Cole asleep?" he asked.

"Yes." Her expression went from genial to concerned.

"You don't have to say it." Nate grabbed the water bottle he'd brought out with him, and drank deeply. Aware they'd known each other only a few days, but were already talking with the candor of two people who had known each other for years, he sighed. "I know I blew it tonight."

Brooke's eyes softened. "That's not what I came over here to say."

Maybe not in those exact words… Disappointed in how he was handling the situation, Nate made no effort to hide his mounting frustration. He wasn't just a CEO, capable of starting a company from scratch and building it into a resounding success, he also had a background in sales. Years of experience honing the winning pitch had schooled him on how to gain the confidence of those who barely knew him. Yet despite all that he was failing mightily with the one person who needed to believe in him most. Failing Landry in the same way Nate himself had been let down in his youth. "Then…what did you want to say?" he asked impatiently.

Brooke perched on the edge of a round, wrought-iron patio table, gripping the edge. "You're pushing him too hard."

As Nate moved closer, the shimmering blue from the swimming pool illuminated the otherwise dark night with a soothing glow. There was enough light for him to see the self-conscious color creeping into her fair cheeks. "All that stuff had to get done today."

Brooke inhaled, the action lifting, then lowering the soft curves of her breasts. A pulse worked in her throat as she kept her eyes meshed with his. "I'm not arguing that."

Nate couldn't say why, he just knew it frustrated and embarrassed him to come up short in front of her. "Then what?" It wasn't as if they could have let Landry continue to go around with his hair in his eyes, wearing clothes he'd long outgrown, when Nate had the power and the means to remedy both.

"I disagree with your timing." Brooke rose gracefully to her feet. "If you want this to work, you have to start looking at the situation from Landry's point of view. Right now he has no say in anything. Grown-ups have decided where he's going to live, and with whom. Two days ago he was residing in his great-grandmother's neighborhood, where he spent all his free time fighting boredom and taking care of her." Brooke looked Nate squarely in the eye. "Now he's in an intellectually challenging summer camp and living here. That's a huge change."

And a good one, Nate thought fiercely, still sure taking Landry in was the right thing to do. "He could be in foster care."

Brooke moved closer. "To him, it's the same thing." She propped her hands on her hips. "I know you're used to just snapping your fingers and making things happen. All CEOs are. But Landry can't just put on a happy face and make this situation work. He's a kid. He needs time to process it, to understand what it is about you that made his mother decide you were the one to bring him up, once his great-grandmother could no longer do so."

"You want me to sing my own praises?" he asked disparagingly.

Brooke leaned toward him. "I want you to pull back, not be so results oriented when it comes to Landry's happiness and his attitude. Just give him space, Nate. Let him be…."

In normal circumstances, Nate would agree with her.

In this particular situation, it sounded like emotional desertion—an action Nate was well-acquainted with, too. "And just hope that he doesn't feel even more abandoned in the process?"

This time it was her turn to concede his point.

"It's a fine line," Brooke said eventually.

"You don't know the half of it," Nate agreed in a flat voice.

"Then tell me," she murmured, her warm tone wrapping him in tenderness.

"My parents are both executives for major corporations." Despite the fact that another wall had just come tumbling down, Nate tried not to make it sound any more important now than it had been then. "Career was everything to them when I was growing up, and it still is."

"You were alone a lot?"

That depended on the definition of alone. Nate finished the last of his water in a single draught. "I always had a nanny. And when I got older, a housekeeper." What he hadn't had were parents who cared as much as he needed them to, then or now.

God help him if he left Landry feeling the same way....

Brooke seemed to intuit all he wasn't saying. Her glance became even more empathetic. She edged close enough that he could inhale the faint citrus fragrance of her skin. "Are your parents still around?"

Nate nodded. "My mother is in China, my dad works in Brussels. Global economy and all that. We get together once a year, usually around Christmas."

"That sounds…"

Cold. It was. Nate turned and looked Brooke in the eye. "I want something different for Landry and me."

This time she smiled. "It'll come." She reached out and

squeezed his hand reassuringly. "You're only just starting to get to know each other right now."

Nate absorbed the heat of her skin pressed against his. Fighting the urge to ditch propriety and take her into his arms, he pointed out, "He's already bonding with you."

Brooke shrugged her slender shoulders. "I'm a mom. He lost a mom. He never really had a dad."

And maybe I don't know how to be one. Nate sighed. Her candor allowed him to say the unspeakable in return. "And maybe Landry doesn't want a dad."

"Maybe not," she said with the wisdom of a woman who had spent years parenting effectively. "But he needs one. He needs you, Nate."

BROOKE HADN'T MEANT THAT to come out that way. Hadn't meant for this conversation to get so personal, so fast. Yet that was what seemed to happen every time she was alone with Nate. They'd find themselves talking about things that were far too intimate for two people who had just met.

"Anyway—" she forced herself to regroup and step away from Nate "—like I said before, that isn't why I came over here."

"So what did you need?" Nate asked curiously.

Talk about a loaded question.

She pushed away the idea of kissing Nate. Just because she had noticed how sexy he looked standing there, with his dark hair rumpled, water still beading on his powerful shoulders, and a beach towel wrapped around his waist, was no reason to be thinking this way.

Brooke swallowed and made herself stay focused on the task, even as she failed to slow her racing pulse. "I came over to borrow a pillow and blanket—I'm low on bedcovers. I didn't anticipate Landry spending the night in the cottage with Cole and me. The boys are occupying both beds…so I'm going to have to sleep on the sofa."

His eyes gleamed in the shadows. "You couldn't have put one of them on the sofa?"

Not without showing favoritism of some kind and causing a problem that way. "It's fine, Nate," Brooke replied. "I can rough it for a night or two."

He shook his head in silent approval. "You're one of a kind, you know."

"Thank you…. I think."

He pivoted and started for the mansion. "Not many women would step up the way you have the past few days."

Brooke fell into step beside him. She had to struggle to keep pace as he swiftly led the way into the house. "You may be underestimating the female species."

Nate paused at the base of the back staircase. "I don't think so."

She tilted her head, not sure what he meant. Only knowing that the words sounded soft and seductive.

So alluring, in fact, that it wasn't as much of a surprise as she would have expected when Nate flattened a hand against her spine, guided her close.

Brooke had plenty of time to pull away.

The surprise was she didn't want to.

She yearned to experience the touch of Nate's lips on hers.

And when it happened, his kiss was everything she had expected—tender and evocative, possessive and masculine. She moaned softly as he threaded his hands through her hair, tangling his tongue with hers. With their mouths fused together, she reveled in the taste of him and the tantalizing fragrance of his aftershave. He was so warm, so solid, so strong. He wanted her so much. She could feel it in the way he pressed against her, urging her to curve her body all the way into his. Brooke hadn't ever felt seduced like this. Or had such a strong yearning to be touched, held, loved. Which was why she had to come up for air. Take a moment. Regain some common sense!

She splayed her hands across his chest. "Nate..."

He lifted his head slightly. He had a dazed, besotted look in his eyes that mirrored the unwanted emotions she harbored deep inside.

"That's been a long time coming," he told her gruffly. And then he kissed her again.

Chapter Five

Brooke had never been one to spend a lot of time kissing. But as Nate pulled her flush against him once again, and delved into the kiss with breathtaking dedication, she began to see what she had been missing. She was light-headed with pleasure as his lips touched one corner of her mouth, then the other, teasingly warm, temptingly reassuring. Her body went soft with pleasure. She wrapped her arms around his neck and tilted her hips into the hardness of his. He made a sound low in his throat and continued kissing her ardently, one hand in her hair, the other coming around to cup her breast.

Engulfed in his touch, in his smell, Brooke felt the possibilities of a liaison with Nate and longed for more. So what if the guy had a string of ex-girlfriends ten miles long? It had been years since she had been wanted like this, or felt like a woman with needs. Years since she had acknowledged the aching void deep inside her.

With his thorough, provocative kisses, Nate brought it all back. The feel of her heart slamming hard against her ribs. The blossoming heat that started in her breasts and spread outward in deep, pulsing waves. The throb of awareness between her thighs, the boneless feeling in her knees. She knew she should play it cool, but when he pursued her like this it was impossible to mask her response. One stroke of his tongue or brush of his finger-tips, and she was trembling all over.

There was something primitive and satisfying about being held against him and savored this way. She could feel his hardness, his need, and knew that whatever normalcy she had been holding on to in his presence was completely gone. There was no point pretending they didn't desire each other, or that his kisses were anything but spectacular. She could only imagine how magnificent his lovemaking would be…if they took this to the next level.

As if hit by the same erogenous thoughts, Nate drew back. Still holding her tightly, he looked down at her. "I could do this all night," he murmured.

"So could I." *If you weren't a client. If I were childless.* Unfortunately, she reminded herself with what little self-discipline remained, she was neither.

With effort, she forced herself to be sensible. "But we both have responsibilities."

For which he apparently cared not a whit, as he continued to stare at her with lust in his eyes.

So she forced herself to say, "Sons to parent." *Emotional baggage still to be dealt with.* "And we can't afford to be distracted."

Finally, she got through to him.

Brought back to reality, Nate inhaled sharply and buried his face against her throat. "And I thought I was the one given to weighing risk," he murmured.

Brooke shifted so that he had to look at her, trying not to think about how good he made her feel. She wasn't sure she followed what he was saying. "In financial terms…in your work?"

"In every way." Their gazes locked and the corner of his

mouth curved upward. "And this," he said, kissing her ever so briefly again, before letting her go, "is a risk worth taking."

BROOKE WAS HALFWAY BACK across the lawn, the borrowed pillow and blanket in her arms, when she saw an ancient Volkswagen pull into Nate's driveway. Her first thought, when she saw a lithe female figure emerge, was that the man who had just kissed her had a visitor.

Her second realization occurred when the woman turned and looked straight at her.

Brooke's heart sank as she recognized the petite auburn-haired grad student with a body that would have given Eva Longoria a run for her money.

"Professor Rylander said I'd find you here," Iris Lomax told Brooke as she neared.

Deciding this conversation should not happen out in public near the caretaker's cottage, Brooke clasped the bedding close to her chest and turned to face her late husband's mistress. "You shouldn't be here," she told Iris. "Especially this late." It was nearly midnight.

"I just got off work. I wait tables to supplement my assistantship. And it couldn't wait." Iris reached into the canvas carryall she had slung over her shoulder. She withdrew an advance copy of Seamus's last book of poetry. "I know you're angry with me for being with your husband, but I can't believe you would stoop this low."

The deep anger in her voice took Brooke aback. "I have no idea what you're talking about."

Iris advanced. "Where do you get off passing off my poems as Seamus's?"

For a second, Brooke was sure she hadn't heard right. "What are you talking about?"

Iris waved the volume with a shaking hand. "Two-thirds of the love poems in Seamus's collection are mine!"

Furiously, she angled a thumb at her chest. "I wrote them! And I helped construct the rest of them, too!"

Brooke could barely breathe. "Surely there's been some mistake."

"You're darn right there has. I'm going to sue Seamus's estate for plagiarism!"

Nate stepped out of the shadows. "How do we know you're telling the truth?"

Brooke was startled by his presence. She'd thought she and Iris were alone.

The grad student sputtered, clearly taken aback. "I've got the originals on my computer!"

Nate stood next to Brooke, silencing Iris with a look. "That doesn't mean anything. You were sleeping with Seamus. You could have copied his work while he was alive. Now that he's gone, you're trying to pass it off as your own."

The woman's jaw dropped.

Brooke was a little surprised, too. She hadn't expected Nate to come to her defense, never mind so gallantly.

"That's not what happened," Iris said heatedly.

In CEO mode once again, Nate withdrew his wallet from his back pocket, took out a business card and handed it to her. "Why don't you gather your proof? Hire an intellectual-property lawyer to represent you. And then call me tomorrow. I'll facilitate a meeting with lawyers for you and Brooke and the publishers."

"The university should be involved, too," Brooke said with a sigh.

Iris glared at her. "Just so you know…I'm not going to let you get away with this. I'm not going to let you and your son benefit financially from my work."

"Believe me, that is the last thing I would ever want to do," Brooke retorted.

Nate draped a comforting arm around Iris's shoulders. "Let me escort you to your car," he murmured.

She relented.

Brooke walked as far as the patio next to the pool, then sat down on a chaise, dropping the bedding beside her.

In the driveway, Nate stood talking with Iris for several minutes. Brooke had no idea what he was saying, but the effect of his words was palpable. When Iris got in her car and finally drove away, it was in a calm, deliberate manner.

Nate returned to Brooke's side. He hunkered down in front of her, took both her hands in hers and searched her face. "Are you okay?"

She gestured impotently, not really sure if she was or not. As she worked to steady her nerves, she said, "I can't believe Seamus did that. And yet…"

"You do?" Nate guessed.

She inhaled deeply and held his gaze. She needed a sounding board. For many reasons, Nate was it. "Seamus had writer's block the last three or four years of his life. No matter how much he tried, he was unable to finish anything. He said he just didn't feel inspired. And then the last year or so, he told me the muse had returned, and he was doing all this great work. It was his excuse for staying away so much, working late."

"You think he was collaborating with Iris?"

"Maybe. She had just started at the university then, as a PhD candidate in poetry. So it's possible he was mentoring her and working with her to improve her writing, and there's just been some confusion about who came up with which lines." Brooke swallowed and forced herself to deal with the worst-case scenario, too. "Then again, maybe what Iris says is true—Seamus was just stealing her words and planning to pass them off as his own all along."

Brooke buried her face in her hands, doing her best to recall. "Whatever happened, the poems for the collection were turned in to Seamus's editor before he died. Nothing has been added or deleted since. The only thing that was done was some very minor editing."

Shifting the pillow and blanket, Nate moved to sit next to her. "It seems like an awfully foolish thing to do. Surely Seamus would have known he would be caught."

That was the logical conclusion for anyone who hadn't possessed illusions of grandeur. Brooke sighed. "Maybe he thought he could 'handle' Iris, if and when she ever found out." Seamus had been known for his ability to lay on the Irish charm. "Or...I don't know. Maybe it wasn't so much the medicine he was taking to help him out in the sack as the stress of the deception that really caused his fatal heart attack. Maybe he was already having an attack of conscience and second thoughts about what he'd done."

"I meant what I said earlier." Nate clasped her hands in his. "I'll help you find an intellectual-property lawyer. I'm sure something can be worked out."

The urge to throw herself in his arms and let him handle everything was almost overwhelming. Knowing she couldn't risk being a passive participant in her life again, even in difficult times like these, she pushed away, bounded to her feet and began to pace. Talking as much to herself as to him, she said, "I have to keep this quiet. I can't let Cole know his father was a fraud. It would destroy him."

Nate paused, his brow furrowed.

It didn't take a body language expert to know what he was thinking. "You don't agree," Brooke surmised.

He gave a small shake of his head. "Cole is a smart kid."

"It would destroy him," Brooke exclaimed, moving

closer. She took his hands once again, gripped them hard. "Promise me, Nate. You'll never breathe a word of this to him."

Nate eyed her reluctant. Finally, he relented, even though she could see he thought it was the wrong move to make. "I promise."

"Mom!" Momentarily disoriented, Brooke opened her eyes and became aware she was stretched out on the living-room sofa of the caretaker's cottage. Early-morning sunshine filtered in through the closed blinds.

Cole waved the volume of poetry and the embossed invitation in front of her face, while Landry lounged in the background, taking in everything.

"Why didn't you tell me Dad had a new book coming out?" Cole demanded. "Even if it was mushy stuff, I would have wanted to see it."

Brooke blinked.

Realizing she must have fallen asleep while perusing the writing, to see if she could figure out if Seamus had actually written any of it or not, she brushed the hair from her eyes and struggled to sit up. Not easy, given how tangled she seemed to be in the blanket she had thrown over herself for warmth.

Landry edged closer, curiosity mixing with the concern on his face.

"I…" Brooke faltered.

"So how come you didn't tell me about this?" Cole repeated intently. As she rubbed the sleep from her eyes, her son plopped down beside her. Too late, Brooke realized she should have hidden the book and invitation away before she fell asleep. Either that or set her alarm, which she had also apparently neglected to do.

"Are we going to the party?" Cole asked eagerly as

Landry roamed the room, his hands stuffed in the pockets of his shorts, as usual. "The invitation is addressed to both of us."

"Yes, it is." Something else she hadn't really noticed when she'd received the invite from Phineas Rylander. But it was fitting, since Cole had attended all Seamus's other book signings.

Brooke cast another look at Landry. "But..."

"So we're going!" Cole beamed.

"No!" She stopped short at the crestfallen look on her son's face, and the perplexed expression on Landry's. Why did Cole choose this morning to look so much like Seamus, especially around the eyes? How was it that Landry knew she was hiding something?

She turned back to her son, shaking off her unease. "I meant..." She faltered again.

"We're not going?" Cole echoed in disbelief.

Brooke held up a hand. Never a morning person to begin with, she felt completely overwhelmed and out of her league today. Especially since she had lain awake half the night worrying about what to do. "Cole, I just..." Guilt and indecision warred within Brooke. Wary of blurting out the wrong thing again, or further alerting Landry to the turmoil roiling inside her, she rose and said beseechingly, "Can you give me a moment to get a cup of coffee?"

Hurt registered on her son's face. "I don't get why you do this."

"Do what?" she asked nervously.

His lower lip trembled. "Act so weird whenever Dad's name comes up, instead of just talking to me about whatever you are worried about!" Cole spun on his heel and bolted out the door. Then came back in to add furiously, "I hate it when you treat me like a little kid who doesn't know anything about anything! 'Cause I am mature enough to go to that book party and not get all bent out of shape just because Dad died and can't be there!"

Brooke latched onto the idea that it was residual grief keeping them from going, rather than the scandal Cole still knew nothing about. She approached her son and put a reassuring hand on his arm. It wouldn't be much longer before he was taller than she was. "Honey, I know it used to be fun when you went with your dad to his poetry readings and book signings. But this wouldn't be the same."

Scowling, Cole clamped his arms over his chest. "Why can't we do what we did at the wake? Have everybody make a toast and remember him fondly?"

Because, Brooke thought, that would only invite someone like Iris Lomax to make a scene. The kind that, thank heaven, had not been made at the funeral, since she had been persuaded by Phineas Rylander not to attend. Now, it was different. Iris had something Professor Rylander did not want revealed, not the other way around. And if it was a university event, there was no way to bar her without raising a lot of eyebrows—and some very fair questions—since she was still a teaching assistant in the English department.

"Why can't we tell stories about Dad and make it fun, Mom?"

Once again, Brooke had to think on the fly. "Because it would be inappropriate. This is a literary function, and I believe they're planning for it to be very stuffy and intellectual—not something either of us would want to sit through for hours on end."

Cole glared at her. "What you really mean is you don't want to go."

What could she say that her son wouldn't see right through, except the truth? "No, honey, I don't."

"Well, I do!" Cole stormed back out of the cottage.

Landry shoved his hands through his newly spiked hair, which actually looked kind of cute, in a disheveled-rock-star kind of way. "You sure blew that one," he commented, his brow arched in adolescent disapproval.

"No kidding," Brooke muttered. She folded the blanket and set it on the pillow, then looked around for her flip-flops. "Stay here," she told him.

Landry seemed to appreciate that directive as much as Cole liked being kept in the dark.

"I'll be back to fix breakfast for you boys in a moment," she added.

Clad in her sleepwear of athletic shorts and a T-shirt, she raced outside. To her dismay she saw that Cole was standing next to Nate, who appeared to have just come back from a run.

She had to admit that Nate's athletic pursuits kept him in really buff shape. Even his legs were amazingly powerful and sexy.

"…so completely unfair," Cole was saying.

Nate wiped the sweat from his face with the hem of his damp, clinging T-shirt. "I'm sure your mom meant to tell you," he soothed.

Brooke joined them. "I just found out about the party yesterday," she said.

"But you had to know this was coming," Cole waved the volume. "Books don't just appear overnight."

He was quoting his father now, Brooke realized.

"Especially poetry books." Cole flipped the hardcover over to look at his father's photo on the dust jacket. "They take years to write and get published."

Brooke turned her gaze away from the handsome face that had fooled her for so many years. "That's true. And I did know the publisher was bringing out a new volume of your dad's poetry." After all, she had signed the contract.

"Then why didn't you tell me?" Cole persisted.

"I wanted it to be a surprise," she said lamely. It wasn't the first time she had lied to Cole to shield him from his father's frailties, but it was the first time she had done so in front of Nate.

The look in Nate's eyes told her what she already knew in her heart—that it was a mistake. "The proceeds from the book are going to be added to your college fund."

Cole seemed mollified. "You still should have showed me the book the moment you got it."

Nate clapped a paternal hand on Cole's shoulder. "Point taken, buddy."

"Hey, I thought you were coming back to make breakfast?" Landry had ambled out to join them.

"Sounds good to me," Nate stated cheerfully. "That is if I'm invited."

Increasing the intimacy between her and her client was not wise—Brooke felt they had already crossed too many boundaries as it was—but right now she really needed the diversion. She flashed an enthusiastic smile. "Absolutely. I'll get those pancakes started right away."

NATE WENT UP TO THE HOUSE to quickly shower and change. By the time he returned, short minutes later, Brooke had breakfast going.

"Did you know my dad?" Landry asked him.

The question came out of left field, and had Nate feeling as off balance as Cole's third degree had left Brooke. Parenting was harder than it looked, Nate realized. Doing his best to be honest and forthright, he nodded. "Yes, I did. Miles Lawrence lived in the same apartment building as me when we were just out of college."

Landry helped himself to a strip of crispy bacon from a plate that had been set on the table. "Did you ever see his stand-up act?"

Nate poured a cup of coffee and lounged against the counter next to Brooke. "A couple of times."

Landry rocked back in his chair. "Was it any good?"

Brooke kept her attention riveted on the pancakes she was cooking.

Nate turned to face the boy. "He was a funny guy."

Hope shone in Landry's eyes. "My mom always said if he'd lived my dad would have been really famous."

Nate forced himself to be generous. "I think she was right."

The teen frowned. "He never married my mom."

It was no comfort, knowing the woman who had shattered Nate's illusion suffered heartbreak, too. "Your great-grandmother told me that." The knowledge had made him sad. If he had wished anything for Seraphina, it was for her to be happy.

Landry broke another strip of bacon in half. He was quiet for a moment. "Do you think that was right?"

This was definitely not getting easier. "I...don't know."

Brooke shot Nate an empathetic look from beneath her lashes, which neither of the boys could see, then swept by him with a plate of steaming hotcakes in hand.

"You're dodging the question," Landry complained.

Warmed by Brooke's steady presence and unspoken support, Nate took another sip of his coffee. "It's complicated."

The instant Brooke set the platter on the table, Landry stacked several golden-brown pancakes on his plate and doused them with maple syrup. He picked up his knife and fork. "If you were the baby daddy, would you marry the baby momma?"

Nate had no doubt whatsoever about that. "Yes."

"Why?" Landry asked with narrowed eyes.

Feeling the warmth of Brooke's approval, Nate answered, "Because I think whenever possible kids should have two parents, a mom and a dad."

Brooke tensed. Although what she could find wanting in that answer, Nate didn't know.

Cole looked over at Brooke, curious now, too. "Do you feel the same way?" He also helped himself to several pancakes.

She nodded and poured more batter on the griddle.

Cole considered that, while he took his first bite. "My dad didn't feel that way," he announced when he had finished chewing. "He said marriage was a trap, and unless I was really in love I should avoid it."

Nate choked in midsip. "You must feel that way, too," Cole said to him, when he'd stopped coughing. "Because you're not married."

Brooke's eyebrows rose. "Cole, for heaven's sake!"

Nate held out a hand, glad this had come up. He wanted to lay it on the line for both boys, set an example. "It's not because I don't want to be," he explained, then paused to look at Brooke, too, before turning his gaze back to them and continuing with heartfelt sincerity. "I want a wife and family more than anything."

Cole and Landry remained skeptical.

"Have you ever been married?" Cole asked.

"No," Nate admitted.

"Engaged?" Landry pressed.

This was more difficult. "Yes," Nate said.

"Who to?" the boy asked curiously.

There was a beat of silence. Aware he couldn't sidestep the question now, Nate confessed, "To your mother."

For a moment, both boys were frozen in shock. Then anger and resentment permeated the room.

"How come nobody ever told me that?" Landry fumed.

"LANDRY HAD A POINT," Brooke said to Nate later, after the boys had disappeared into their rooms to get ready for summer camp. She and Nate had seized the opportunity to step outside with their second cup of coffee and engage in some private conversation. "Someone should have told him about the relationship between you and his mother."

Nate didn't like receiving criticism that was ill-founded, but in this case it was worth enduring, since he needed a sounding board. "I assumed someone had."

Brooke paused, mug halfway to her lips. "You don't mind the questions it's going to create?"

He shrugged. "They would have come up anyway." Kids were curious. Heck, *he* was curious. About Brooke in general…and specifically, in whatever she'd put into those pancakes to make them taste so good. They were hands down the best he had ever eaten. And he'd dined in some mighty fine places over the years.

Brooke's delicately shaped brows knit together. She hadn't had a chance to get dressed in the clothes or put on the subtle make up that comprised her work armor. Her slightly tousled hair and bare lips made her seem more accessible. She twisted her mouth in disagreement. "You don't know that."

Nate knew avoiding problems never worked, in business or at home. He wouldn't pretend otherwise, even to score points with a woman he found more sexually attractive with every second that passed.

He walked a little farther from the house. "I know I'm not going to hide the truth from him."

Brooke sauntered after him, not stopping until they had reached the waterfall in the lagoon-style swimming pool. She looked up at him, bewilderment lighting her eyes. "You'd really tell him you're unsure about his paternity?"

Nate wouldn't enjoy doing so, but the way he saw it, he had no choice. Not if he wanted Landry to trust him. "If and when he asks, yes."

Her expression grew troubled. "You don't know how he would react."

Nate was beginning to see how Brooke would react. "Then I guess we'd find out."

She blew out a gusty breath. "It could hurt him, Nate."

He raised an eyebrow. "Being lied to or deliberately misled would hurt him more."

The door to the cottage opened. Both boys tramped out, backpacks over their shoulders. "Mom! Camp! We're going to be late!" Cole called.

"Why don't I take them today?" Nate offered.

Brooke looked at the kids, who both shrugged. She turned back to Nate, gratitude in her eyes. "I'd appreciate the help this morning," she said.

"Then let's get a move on," Nate told the guys.

He wanted to spend time with them, and then get back to Brooke.

BROOKE WATCHED THEM all amble off toward Nate's Jaguar sedan, then she hit the shower. When she finally headed over to the main house to await the arrival of the moving crew, Nate was just coming down the sweeping front stairs. Since returning from taking the kids to camp, he'd changed out of the casual slacks and shirt he'd put on after his run. In a dove-gray business suit, coordinating shirt and tie, he looked handsome enough to take her breath away. He smelled great, too, she couldn't help but note as he crossed to her side. As if he'd taken time to slap on some of that leather-and-spice cologne after he shaved. "So what's happening here today?" he asked.

Brooke put her hormones on ice and switched to businesswoman mode. "The auctioneer and I are going to do an inventory of everything you're sending over to be sold. And then the house is going to be emptied out."

"Except for my bedroom and the library," Nate said. His gaze drifted over her as he favored her with a rakish smile.

Insides humming, Brooke nodded. "Those will remain as is."

"For now," he added. "I'm going to want my bedroom changed out eventually, too."

"No problem." She consulted her clipboard as she pushed away a mental image of Nate lounging between the sheets. It was not something she would likely ever see. She lifted her head again and looked into his eyes. "We'll just have to sit down and go over what you want."

And we won't think about what I want.

Which is a man like you in my life.

Nate glanced at his watch. "How about today?" Pulling the BlackBerry from his suit jacket, he checked the calendar. "Can you meet with me at my office downtown? Say around one o'clock?"

Brooke tried not to think how good it felt to be standing here with him like this. "Sure." He was a client, and that was all.

He flashed a disarming smile and touched her gently on the arm. "Then I'll see you then."

Chapter Six

"What's going on here?" Dan Kingsland asked, four hours later.

Nate paused in the door of the conference room where a private lunch had been set up. Resting beside his place setting was the palette of paint colors Brooke had given him to peruse. Good. Everything was exactly as he'd wanted. Glad his business with his partners had been concluded, he turned back to the guys as he attempted to usher them out. "It's a lunch meeting."

Grady McCabe eyed the china and silver. "You never set out roses for us when you invite us here to dine with you," he ribbed.

"We usually get take-out containers and no tablecloth," Jack Gaines remarked.

"And you never mix business with courtship," Travis Carson observed. "So who is this lady who's prompting you to break your own rules? And where is she?"

Nate knew the fastest way to get rid of his friends was to tell them the truth and send them on their merry way. "It's Brooke Mitchell."

The guys chorused approval with big grins. "Ah, the home makeover expert," Travis said.

"Sure she's not making over you, too?" Dan drawled.

"Or just making do," Jack joked.

Nate winced. "Funny."

"Seriously, Nate," Grady said, "don't even think about adding Ms. Mitchell to your string of broken hearts. 'Cause if you do, Alexis will have your hide."

"Make that all our wives," Dan warned. "Emily, Holly and Caroline are friends with Brooke, too. They won't take kindly to you flirting with her, then deciding she's not The One, either."

Nate had been given a bad rap in that regard. "I don't do that," he argued.

More than one of the guys grunted skeptically. "You're pretty picky," Grady observed.

Nate frowned. "I don't want to invest in the wrong relationship again." This time he needed to approach love with the same caution and thoughtfulness he managed his business, and connect with the right woman first. Then and only then would he allow himself to get more involved.

The fact that Brooke seemed like the right woman put him one step closer to his goal of having the loving, supportive family he had always wanted—and never had.

"Maybe no one told you?" Dan chided. "Women don't come with any guarantees."

Travis held up a hand. "Relax, guys. From what I understand, Brooke is every bit as romance-shy as our pal here."

That was true, Nate silently acknowledged. And clearly it was going to make moving forward in his pursuit of her even harder.

A knock sounded on the door. Looking as gorgeous as ever in a lemon sheath and short-sleeved white cardigan, Brooke stuck her head in. "Am I interrupting?"

"Not at all." Grady gave his friends a look that told them to exit ASAP. He turned back to Brooke. "Our meeting is done."

But she was not done talking to his pals. She sauntered in and set her leather carryall on the floor next to the table. "I have to tell you guys, One Trinity River Place is amazing. You should be very proud of yourselves."

Nate's partners beamed. "Go on," Jack urged.

"Yeah," Grady teased with his typical "if you've done it it ain't bragging" attitude. "We can take it."

An appreciative light sparkled in Brooke's pretty eyes. "Okay, Grady, you get kudos for putting together the development deal that made the high-rise possible. Dan deserves 'em for designing the skyscraper, Travis for constructing it. And I'd be remiss if I didn't single out Jack for making sure all communications and electronics are state-of-the-art high tech. And last but not least, Nate—" Brooke paused, her eyes locking with his for an extra long second "—for having a business that is so successful you can afford to house it in a place as luxurious as this."

And here Nate had thought she wasn't impressed with all he had accomplished, building a multimillion dollar company from scratch!

"Ever thought of going into public relations?" Travis teased.

Dan winked. "We could use you on our team."

Brooke grinned, enjoying the banter and camaraderie with the guys as much as Nate was. Unfortunately, their time together was limited. And when he had the opportunity, he wanted her all to himself. "She has a job," Nate reminded them. "Which she is trying to do, if you guys would all clear out of here."

Hands raised in surrender all around. "We get the hint."

Nate shut the door behind his pals after they filed out. "Sorry."

For the first time, Brooke seemed to take in the details

of their surroundings. "I didn't realize we'd be doing lunch here."

Telling himself that was not disapproval in her golden-brown eyes, Nate ushered her toward the table and held out her chair. "It's an environment that is more conducive to work."

WAS IT? BROOKE WONDERED. Looking at the table set for two, in a private room with a spectacular view of downtown Fort Worth, all she could think about was what it would be like to have a date with the handsome CEO.

Not that he was asking for anything but help with Landry and in redecorating his home, but he had kissed her. And those kisses had stayed with her like nothing ever had before.

Which was exactly why she shouldn't allow herself to be distracted this way. Business was business, and this meeting today should be all about his home makeover, she reminded herself.

Brooke settled into the chair Nate offered. "Then let's get down to it."

He sat opposite her.

"Have you had a chance to look at the color palettes I gave you this morning?" she asked.

"I liked them all."

And I like you. But she was digressing again…. She forced herself to return to business. "That's not exactly the response I was looking for."

After they exchanged smiles, Nate gestured. "I can't make a decision about something like that."

He seemed genuinely lost at sea. Brooke leaned toward him and soothed, "You probably have stronger opinions than you realize."

The lift of his black brow said he doubted it.

She brought out a notepad and pen. "Describe a space you really like," she suggested.

Mischief turned up the corners of his lips. "The caretaker's cottage. Since you made it over, it's very...I don't know." He struggled visibly for the correct terms. "Serene...calming...yet cheerful and homey."

"I started with a neutral base—the sand-colored paint that was already on the walls. Added durability and texture with the washable denim slipcovers, and brought in splashes of color with the rugs, bedcovers and other accessories."

Nate thought a moment. "Let's do the same thing in the main house."

"Sounds good. Any colors you truly detest?" She struggled not to notice how sexy and self-assured he looked.

"Orange and purple. Lime green."

Same with me, she thought. Although she had done spaces in those colors for clients. "What about styles of furnishings?" she asked crisply.

"Nothing dainty," he specified. "Everything should be comfortable and kid friendly."

Got it. Brooke made another note. "What about your bedroom?"

Nate shrugged, not the least bit interested. "We'll do that last," he said. "But you should probably talk to Landry about what he wants and get started on his bedroom right away."

And now for the bad news... "I tried last night," Brooke said with a wince.

Nate tensed. "And...?"

As much as Brooke wanted to protect Nate, she couldn't. If he was going to help Landry adjust, he had to know where things stood. She put down her pen and reluctantly shared, "He told me not to worry about it. He didn't think he'd be staying with you for long. He said bunking in the guest cottage was fine."

Nate's face registered the same disappointment Brooke had felt at the time of the exchange.

"He'll come around." She reached across the table and briefly squeezed Nate's hand. Fingers tingling from contact, she took a deep breath and sat back, counseling gently, "You have to give him time. In the meantime, it might help if he went to see his great-grandmother."

The brooding look was back on Nate's handsome face. "I think so, too. I offered to take him this morning, when I was driving the boys to camp." His lips compressed. "He declined."

Brooke played with her fork. "Maybe it shouldn't be an option."

An unreadable emotion appeared in Nate's blue eyes. "That was my first instinct," he admitted slowly. "And then I got to thinking, we're already forcing him to do so much. Maybe Jessalyn is right. Maybe Landry shouldn't see her again until he accepts the reality of the situation and settles in a bit."

"And maybe," Brooke countered equably, "what he needs is to see her, so he'll finally understand this is all for the best."

Nate's BlackBerry buzzed. He glanced at the screen. "Percy Dearborn is waiting to see us."

Brooke lifted a brow, confused.

"He's an intellectual-property lawyer—the best in the area."

She did a double take. "Excuse me?"

The CEO was back full force. "I assumed you wouldn't have time to find someone, so I made a few phone calls this morning."

As if it was the most natural thing in the world to

do for a woman you'd just become acquainted with and kissed…

Nate leaned back in his chair and forged on. "I told him the situation and he offered to represent you and your late husband's estate in the plagiarism claim being made by Iris Lomax. It's important we go on the offense here."

Memories of similar situations surfaced. "This isn't your situation to manage!"

His eyes narrowed. "You need help."

Brooke had been trying not to think about that. Dealing with Iris's sudden reappearance in her life had been disturbing enough. "Then I'll find it on my own," she insisted.

"*Have* you hired anyone?" Nate pressed.

"No, but…"

Determination tautened his jaw. "Do you want Cole to see this played out in the newspapers?"

Brooke flushed. "Of course not."

Nate rose and moved around to pull out her chair. "Then I suggest you meet with Percy and get his advice on how to proceed." He touched her shoulder gently. "You can give me hell later."

Brooke glared at Nate. "We will talk about this," she promised.

"Of that," Nate said drily, "I have no doubt."

Brooke spent the next half hour answering Percy Dearborn's steady stream of questions. Finally, he put down his pen. "I do not think the court would find you personally liable, given the fact that you were in no way involved in the writing, preparation or submission of the manuscript, which was all done by your late husband prior to his demise. The estate, however, could be found liable, if the proof of theft that Ms. Lomax alleges does exist. Because you did follow through on getting the work published, as your late husband wished."

Brooke's throat tightened with dread. She folded her hands in her lap, glad she had Nate sitting beside her to offer support. She looked at the distinguished attorney. "What do you suggest I do?"

"I'd like to meet with Ms. Lomax and her lawyer, get a look at her proof, and if that holds up, see if we can't come to some kind of settlement before a lawsuit is filed and the matter becomes public."

Brooke relaxed slightly. "What about the university?"

"I'll talk to Phineas Rylander as soon as we know what the situation is."

"Thank you."

"It's no problem." The attorney stood and put his laptop computer back in the carrying case. "That's what we lawyers are here for. To help straighten out messes like this."

Brooke shook his hand, then waited while Nate walked him out.

She was standing at the window in Nate's private office, looking down at the Trinity River, when he returned. "Okay," he said, bracing his hands on his waist and pushing back the edges of his suit coat. "Let me have it with both barrels."

Why did he have to be so reasonable? Brooke wondered. It was charm like his that had gotten her into hot water in the first place.

"I get the fact that you like to manage things," she told him quietly, "but we need to be clear about something. You are *never* to jump in like that and take control of my life again."

NATE KNEW THE PRUDENT thing to do was simply to agree with Brooke. Unfortunately, he could not do that in good conscience. His integrity required he be honest with her. "If I see you making a mistake, hiding from the truth, I'm going to speak up."

"There's a difference between speaking up and telling me I'm wrong, and going out and hiring a lawyer for me."

Knowing he had to touch her or go crazy, Nate tucked his hand in hers and rubbed a thumb over the back of her hand. "I told you last night I would help you find someone to handle this for you."

Color highlighted her elegant cheeks. "I expected you to ask around and give me some names," she blurted. "Not actually set up an appointment with Percy Dearborn without speaking to me first." She paused, her silence filled with a mixture of disappointment and disillusionment. "I get that you were trying to help, but that was over the line, Nate."

He felt like he had when he was a kid and his parents were unhappy with him, despite the fact that he had done his level best to accomplish whatever it was that needed to be done.

And yet he knew the depth of his protectiveness would have been unwarranted, had he not been so interested in Brooke. "Point taken," he said finally, aware that he was rushing her and shouldn't be. "I should have consulted you first." Should have adopted a gentler, more patient approach.

Brooke peered up at him. "Why does my dilemma matter so much to you anyway?" she queried softly, searching his eyes.

Nate brushed a strand of hair from her cheek and tucked it behind her ear. "I didn't want to see you and Cole get hurt. I could tell from the look on your face that all you wanted to do was ignore the threat and wait for the trouble to blow over. And I know from personal experience how badly that always turns out."

Looking as beautiful as she did vulnerable, Brooke gave him a quizzical glance. Her encouragement prompted him to continue. "On some level I knew there was more going on with Seraphina and Miles Lawrence than she said, but I had a lot of reasons for not dealing with the situation the way I should have." Nate recited them wearily. "I was busy building my business. We were engaged. I loved her. I didn't want anything getting in the way of our marriage."

Brooke tightened her fingers around his. "Don't tell me you blame yourself for what Seraphina did," she murmured.

How could he not? It took two people to make a relationship succeed, to make it fail. Nate shrugged and admitted ruefully, "Had I paid attention to the signs, given her the attention she obviously needed, she might have never run off with Miles."

Brooke's eyes glittered as she jumped to his defense. "And maybe she would have anyway," she said. "Maybe the failing was hers and hers alone."

Wishing Brooke wasn't working for him, so he could go ahead and pursue her the no-holds-barred way he wanted to, Nate studied her. "Is that the way you feel about Seamus?"

She sighed. "I was a good wife. I loved him. I gave him everything I had and he cheated on me when he should have respected our marriage vows and been loyal to me and our son," she reflected sadly. "And now it's possible he cheated Iris Lomax, too, by stealing her work and passing it off as his own. Is it what Iris deserves, for carrying on with a married man? I don't know. The only thing I'm certain about is that I am not taking the blame for my late husband's lack of character. And you shouldn't blame yourself for what your ex did, either," Brooke told Nate pointedly. "Because the moral failing was hers and hers alone. Unless...you've cheated on someone, too?"

Ah, the test he had been expecting, given his undeserved reputation as a womanizer. "I would never do that," he told her quietly.

Their gazes meshed. "Neither would I," she said.

Nate smiled and took her other hand in his. "Then it seems we have that in common," he said, looking down at her.

Brooke smiled at him briefly, then withdrew her hands and stepped back. "Just don't try and boss me around or take over my life," she warned, all feisty, independent single mom and accomplished businesswoman. "Because I am perfectly capable of looking after myself."

BROOKE'S PARTING SHOT haunted Nate for the rest of his day. He knew she was a capable woman. He also knew she was in a weak position, legally and personally, and it was that vulnerability, the sense that she needed him as much as he needed her, that made him want to protect her.

The question was, how could he make her see that his concern was something to be appreciated instead of resented? That it was okay for a woman to accept help from the man in her life, and vice versa? And that was what he wanted to be, he realized. The man in her life.

Kissing her again would remind her of the chemistry they had felt. Maybe further develop intimacy and passion between them.

But that, too, was hard to accomplish when they had two chaperones on the premises every evening.

Nevertheless, Nate knew that where there was a will, there was a way.

In the meantime, he had told Brooke that he would retrieve the boys from summer camp and pick up some Texas barbecue on the way home, so he headed out.

"How was camp?" Nate asked, when the boys got in his Jaguar.

"Really cool," Cole answered, and proceeded to talk about the computer video game he was designing. Landry was working on a similar project. And they were still chattering about the problems and successes with their designs when they got home.

"Sounds like you're both learning a lot," Brooke observed over dinner.

Landry smiled at Brooke. He finished his mouthful of brisket and forked up some potato salad. "I really like the fencing lessons, too. It's a lot harder than it looks...."

"I'll bet." Brooke flashed an understanding, appreciative grin. As Landry basked in her approval, Nate saw how much the teen needed a maternal presence in his life again.

Almost as much as Nate himself needed this particular woman to stay in his life...

"I know what you're thinking," Brooke murmured, when he stayed behind to help her clean up after the boys went off to shoot hoops on the sport court at the rear of the property.

Glad for the time alone with her, he carried the dishes to the sink and gathered up the empty take-out containers. "And what is that?" he teased.

Brooke placed the leftovers in airtight bags and slid them into the fridge, then turned around to face him. Leaning against the fridge, she answered drily, "The same thing *I* think when I see Cole looking at you like you are some kind of superhero. It's not enough reason for us to get together."

Nate set aside what he was doing and slowly crossed the distance between them. He stopped in front of her and braced a forearm on either side of her slender shoulders.

He hadn't intended to make another move on her right here and now, but then again, he hadn't intended a lot of things when it came to Brooke Mitchell.

"Then how about this?" he offered softly, leaning in to kiss her again.

Chapter Seven

Brooke knew allowing Nate to put the moves on her wasn't
the wisest course of action. But sometimes, she thought
wistfully as his lips settled ever so nicely over hers, being
cautious wasn't all it was cracked up to be.

Sometimes a gal had to just go with the dictates of
fate.

And fate had put her right here, right now, with Nate.

So what if it wasn't meant to last? Or if they were drawn
together solely by their mutual need for support, guidance
and assistance?

They were here. Now. Together. They had maybe five
minutes to enjoy the dreamy passion of their kiss, and the
encapsulating warmth of his hard body pressed up against
hers.

Five minutes to forget—even for one moment—that...
Wait! Were those footsteps racing down the hall...toward
them?

Apparently so, Brooke realized, since Nate heard them,
too.

He broke off the kiss, stepped back.

She swung open the refrigerator door and ducked behind
it, just in the nick of time.

The pounding footsteps hit the porcelain tile and swept

into the kitchen. "The ball's low on air," Cole announced, holding up an orange globe with black edging.

"Yeah. We figured you probably had an air pump somewhere," Landry added.

Brooke finished smoothing her hair and blotting her mouth. Composure restored as much as possible, she closed the fridge and stepped back. To her relief, Nate looked more relaxed than she felt.

He shot her a reassuring, we'll-pick-this-up-again-later glance that only she could see, then turned back to the boys. "The air pump is in the garage. Let's go out together so I can show you how it works."

NATE GOT THE BOYS SET UP, shot a few hoops with them, then headed back to the main house. Halfway there, he got a phone call from work, alerting him to a problem that needed to be addressed right away. It took an hour to work things out. No sooner had he hung up than Landry appeared at the library door. Dressed in a pair of jersey shorts, a T-shirt and flip-flops, his damp, spiky hair standing on end, he looked like he had just come out of the shower.

"Got a minute?" he asked.

Wondering if it was his imagination or if the teen had grown taller in the last few days, Nate nodded. "Come on in."

Landry shut the door behind him. "I was wondering if you still had pictures of my mom and you, when the two of you were together."

Good question, and one that caught Nate off guard. He gestured for him to have a seat. "I returned her stuff when our engagement ended."

Landry perched on the edge of the black leather sofa.

"So you don't have anything." His shoulders sagged in disappointment.

Nate spun around in his swivel chair, so they were facing each other. "If you're talking about old love letters or anything like that, no. But I might have some photos that escaped the postbreakup purge."

He turned back to his desk, disconnected from his company's network and opened up the drive that held all his personal information. Within it were files of photos that he'd scanned into memory, arranged chronologically.

He went back sixteen years, to the month he had first started dating Seraphina. The personal photos of the two of them were gone, but Landry's mom was in a number of his company photos. "Here she is at the second annual company picnic." Back then, Nate had employed only a dozen people, so it was easy to spot her.

Landry flattened his hands on the desktop and leaned in for a closer look. "Wow. She looks young."

And happy…as did Nate. He smiled, remembering that time in his life when it seemed he was going to get everything he wanted in short order, including the "happy family" of his dreams.

He scrolled through more photos. "And here she is at that year's 5k race to raise funds for cancer research."

Landry pulled up a chair close to Nate, so he could better view the screen. He propped his elbows on the desk and leaned in again. "Do you think she had any idea she would have cancer herself one day?"

"No. She just did that to help others."

Landry smiled fondly, reflecting. "She was good that way."

Nate found half a dozen more photos of him and Seraphina—all at company events, all with other people. He hadn't noticed it at the time, but as he studied their body language now, he could see what he had been blind to then. Subtly but surely, he and Seraphina had been growing apart as his success and the company grew.

Finally, they got to the last week he and Seraphina had officially been a couple. Nate clicked on the photo. "I think this is the last one I have," he said.

They had been with a group of friends at a New Year's Eve party at a swank hotel downtown. Dress was formal. Seraphina looked incredibly beautiful. And unhappy, even in her cardboard top hat, with a paper whistle in her hand.

Landry studied the numbers printed on the Happy New Year banner. "This was fifteen years ago," he said.

Nate nodded. "We broke up the following week."

Landry blinked. "You know, my birthday is in mid-August. Eight months later."

Nate swore to himself. He'd been so busy tripping down memory lane, he hadn't thought about Landry doing the math. He swallowed and aimed for reassuringly casual. "Yeah."

"So I could be *your* kid?" The boy's eyes widened.

Wasn't that the fifty-thousand-dollar question? "I don't know," Nate said finally, wishing he did. He forced himself to meet Landry's searching eyes. "It…possible." There was no clue from the way Landry looked. He had his mother's hair and eye color. His features were an amalgam. His height he could have gotten from either Nate or Miles Lawrence.

Landry stood and began to prowl the room restlessly. "But you don't know for certain." His flip-flops slapped on the geometric patterned rug.

Nate wished he had the right to take him in a hug and comfort him the way he had seen his friends comfort their sons, the way his own father had never comforted him.

But he didn't. Because he knew that to push Landry into something else he wasn't ready for would be to lose the rapport they had managed to build thus far.

Aware he deserved an honest answer, Nate exhaled slowly. "No...I don't know for certain."

Hurt and confusion shone in Landry's blue-gray eyes. "Is that why you were so interested in becoming my guardian and adopting me?" He ran a hand across the peach fuzz on his face. "Because you think I'm yours?"

Nate reminded himself to get Landry a razor. He didn't even know if the boy had one. "I agreed to become your guardian and adopt you because it's what your mother wanted."

Landry's jaw thrust out pugnaciously. "What about what you and I want?"

Nate stood. He closed the distance between them in two strides and put his hand on Landry's shoulder. "This *is* what I want."

"Sure." Landry jerked away. "*If* I'm your kid." He stared at Nate, a muscle working in his jaw. "What if I'm not?"

Nate regarded him evenly. "You will be when the adoption is final."

Another tense silence ticked out. Landry stood as if braced for battle, still glaring. "You're telling me you don't want to find out?"

They were dealing with a time bomb here. Nate knew he could handle the results, whatever they were. He wasn't sure Landry could weather them half as well. And that being the case... Nate gestured noncommittally. "I don't see the point." It wouldn't change what happened in the end. Landry would still end up being adopted by him. Landry would be his son; he would be Landry's father.

"Well, I sure do." The teen threw up both hands in

barely suppressed fury. "I want a DNA test." The words were flat, final.

Nate struggled to calm him down. "Landry—"

"I have to know."

Nate could see that was so. In his place, he admitted to himself reluctantly, he would probably feel the same way. So he tackled the problem the way he did all others, head-on. "All right."

"So you'll arrange it?" Landry pressed, coming closer once more as he sought to extract a promise.

It was all Nate could do not to pull the kid into a hug. With a nod, he vowed, "First thing tomorrow."

BROOKE WAS LOADING clothes into the washer when Landry burst back into the caretaker's cottage. His face was a blotchy pink and white as he brushed past her, heading toward his bedroom. "Landry?" She dropped what she was doing and went after him. "What's wrong? What happened?"

"Ask Nate!" He slammed the door behind him.

Cole came out of the bathroom, smelling like soap and still drying his hair. "What's going on?" he asked in concern.

"I'm not sure," Brooke murmured, torn between going to Landry and talking to Nate first. Forewarned was forearmed. And right now she was leery of doing and saying the wrong thing and making an already bad situation worse. "Would you mind hanging here while I go talk to Nate?"

"No problem." Cole hesitated outside the shut bedroom door. "You think I should try?"

The door opened, and Landry appeared. He looked at Cole. "You can come in," he said tersely, glancing at Brooke as if she was an enemy. "That's it."

Okay. Now she *really* had to talk with Nate. "I'll be back in a few minutes, guys," she said. "You know where I'll be, so come and get me if you need me."

"Right, Mom." Cole's eyes were trained toward his friend.

The bedroom door shut.

Brooke slid her feet into her clogs and headed out across the lawn.

Nate was standing on the stone terrace that ran along the rear of the mansion. Hands gripping the balustrade, he was looking toward the cottage.

Slowly, he came to meet Brooke. She mounted the steps as quickly as possible. "What did he say?" Nate asked.

His usual self-assurance was gone.

Brooke's heartbeat accelerated as she closed the distance between them. "Nothing illuminating. What happened?"

Nate exhaled. Weary lines bracketed his eyes. "Landry wanted to see some photos of his mother and me. The last one was taken on New Year's Eve, right before we broke up. He read the banner, did the math. Figured out his paternity was somewhat in question."

Brooke caught her breath. "You didn't…"

"Lie to him?" Nate stiffened, letting her know she had struck a nerve. "No. I didn't. Which is why he now wants a DNA test."

Her eyes widened. "And you agreed?"

Nate's jaw set in that stubborn way she was beginning to know so well. "Landry wants to know the truth. I get that."

But did he get the rest of it? Brooke wondered, her years of parenting coming to the fore and giving her a broader view of the situation. "You understand," she told him, as gently as possible, "that however this turns out, you're in trouble."

Nate quirked a brow. "For telling the truth?"

Forcing herself to ignore the edge in his voice, she continued, "If Landry is your biological son, it means his birth certificate is a lie, and his mother lied to both of you all these years. And if he isn't, then…" Brooke lifted her hands helplessly. "That's got to hurt now, too."

Because it meant Nate and Landry would never have that biological connection every parent and child wanted, whether they admitted it or not.

Nate sighed and shoved a hand through his hair. "Obviously, it's not a situation I'd want." He turned gleaming blue eyes to hers. "But I'm not going to run from it or encourage Landry to do so, either. Whatever the situation turns out to be, it's best we deal with it now."

Another silence fell, this one even more packed with emotion. Nate studied her. "You don't agree?"

I think you're headed for a long, hard fall. And so is Landry. But aware she had already overstepped her bounds in giving her opinion, she shrugged. "It's not really up to me, is it?"

His mouth curved downward and he shook his head. "No, I guess it's not."

Another long, uncomfortable silence fell.

Hard to believe, Brooke thought, that just a couple of hours ago they had been standing in his kitchen making out like a couple on the threshold of taking the next big step….

Hard to believe she had put so much in jeopardy, so fast.

Which was why she had to take charge of her life once again. And control what she could of a situation that was fast becoming an emotional mess. "But there is

3 Months Free

when you subscribe for 12 Months

SAVE OVER £41

SEE OVERLEAF
FOR DETAILS

www.millsandboon.co.uk/subscriptions

SAVE OVER £41

Subscribe to Cherish today to get 5 stories
a month delivered to your door for 12 months,
saving a fantastic £41.70

Alternatively, subscribe for 6 months and save
£16.68, that's still an impressive 20% off!

FULL PRICE	YOUR PRICE	SAVINGS	MONT
£166.80	£125.10	25%	12
£83.40	£66.72	20%	6

As a welcome gift we will also
send you a FREE L'Occitane
gift set worth £10

**PLUS, by becoming a member you
will also receive these additional benefits:**

- 🌹 FREE P&P Your books delivered to your
  door every month at no extra charge
- 🌹 Be the first to receive new titles two
  months ahead of the shops
- 🌹 Exclusive monthly newsletter
- 🌹 Excellent Special offers
- 🌹 Membership to our Special Rewards programme

No Obligation- You can cancel your subscription at any time by writing
to us at Mills & Boon Book Club, PO Box 676, Richmond. TW9 1WU.

To subscribe, visit
www.millsandboon.co.uk/subscriptions

MILL
BOO

S1

something that is up to me. And that's our…attraction to each other."

Nate folded his arms across his broad chest and waited. With his black hair tousled, and a hint of beard lining his face, he looked wildly sexy.

"It can't continue." Brooke felt her throat tighten, but pushed on. "We can't let the kids see us kissing."

"I think they could handle it," Nate replied with a grin.

"They could handle seeing two random people kissing," Brooke countered, as her heart somersaulted inside her chest. "But you and me…?" Surreptitiously, she wiped her perspiring palms on the sides of her shorts. "I think it sends the wrong message."

"Which would be?"

She gulped, aware she was the one now on a road she never should have taken. "That it's okay to become casually involved with someone you're working for."

"First of all…" Nate's glance raked her appreciatively from head to toe. His voice dropped a husky notch. "There's nothing casual about the way I feel when I kiss you. And if you're honest with yourself, there's nothing casual about the way you feel, either."

Brooke's face heated. He had scored a point with that one. Wise or not, their kisses were hot!

"Second," he continued, looking deep into her eyes, "in another week or so you won't be working this job."

Which meant she wouldn't be here all the time. And then where would they stand? Would Nate still pursue her this intensely, or would she merely be out of sight, out of mind? The thought that she was about to hook up with another Casanova filled her with dread and made her want to pull back even more, to protect herself. "Exactly my point," she reiterated.

His shoulders tautened. "So what's the problem?"

Irritated at the continued need to spell out her objections for him, in great detail, Brooke retorted, "The problem is Landry is missing a mom and Cole is missing a dad. They like it when the four of us hang out together and have dinner and stuff, and when I'm not here that won't be happening anymore." Cole would miss it as much as she would. Probably Landry, too.

Nate regarded her, incredulous. "Who says?"

Brooke took a deep breath and let it out slowly. "You know what I mean."

He dropped his arms and moved in. "I know you're trying to put up boundaries that will keep us from getting any closer." He caught her by the arms and held her in place when she would have bolted. "It's not going to work." He lowered his gaze to her mouth, before returning it ever so slowly to her eyes. She stilled, fighting the riptide of desire churning through her. "Landry is bonding with you," Nate continued in a quiet, admiring voice. "And so am I. And Cole's important to me, too." He coaxed her closer still. "There's no getting away from that."

No getting away from how she felt whenever they were close like this.

Brooke paused and wet her lips. "I still don't want them to know that…"

"We've kissed?" He finished her sentence for her. "And that I want to make love to you?"

Brooke felt her stomach drop. "Just say what's on your mind, why don't you?" she muttered wryly.

Her attempt to deflect the emotions with a deadpan remark failed.

Nate only grew more serious. "I told you, Brooke. I believe in putting the truth out there, whatever it is. Ignoring feelings never accomplished anything."

Clearly, he wanted to kiss her again as much as she wanted to kiss him. And if it hadn't been for the two kids, the potential for hurt, Brooke knew she would have thrown caution to the wind. Fortunately, for all their sakes, she had a mission to fulfill.

"Honesty is always the best policy," Nate continued.

She thought about the hurt, confused look in Landry's eyes just now. And worse, what could be coming up. She splayed her hands across the solid warmth of Nate's chest, forcing distance between them. "You're wrong, Nate," she told him softly. "The best thing we can do is *protect* our kids. And make sure they don't have to deal with anything they shouldn't have to deal with. So I need your promise." She pushed free of his embrace. "No more kissing me when the boys are anywhere in the vicinity." She took a deep breath. "No more kissing me at all."

Nate's eyes darkened. "I agree to the first," he said, with the self-assured authority he probably used in board meetings. "Not to the latter."

Brooke blinked.

He regarded her with a mixture of resignation and amusement. "Yeah, I know you're used to calling the shots. You've made that perfectly clear." He flashed a wicked, challenging smile as he came closer once again, and chucked her beneath the chin. "But I like to call the shots, too. And what my gut is telling me is that this connection we feel is something special enough to pursue. And that, sweetheart, is exactly what I plan to do."

"EARTH TO BROOKE?" Holly Carson said, from the opposite end of the mansion's vast dining room at nine the next morning.

Brooke started. She hadn't been with it since she'd dropped Cole at camp and Nate and Landry had left for the doctor's office. She shook off her mental fog and headed toward the talented artist, who also happened to be the wife of Nate's business partner and good friend Travis Carson. "Sorry."

"You asked me to come here this morning to give you my opinion about using murals to break up the dining room into a more usable space, and all you've done is stare glumly out the window."

Brooke flashed an apologetic smile. "I'm sorry. I'm distracted."

"And no wonder." Holly looked around at the big, echoing space. "It's a huge job."

Brooke forced her mind back to business. "So what do you think?"

Holly paced back and forth, studying the light coming in through the tall windows. "That you're right. It would really help to put something on the wall at each end of the space, with a neutral-colored break in between."

They discussed possible themes, then walked toward the kitchen, where Holly's husband, Travis, and another business partner of Nate's, Dan Kingsland, were already taking measurements.

For the next fifteen minutes, they discussed how to replace the utilitarian, stainless steel work island in the center of the room with something warmer and more family friendly. Dan, an architect, was going to do the design. The custom-cabinetry arm of Travis's construction company would build and install the final product to match the existing wood cabinets. Marble countertops would be added—again by Travis's company—to further dress up the space.

They were just finishing when Nate walked in. All eyes turned to him.

"The DNA test go okay?" Travis asked.

Nate nodded. "We'll get the results in seven to ten days."

Holly held her sketch pad to her chest. With the comforting tone of a mother who had successfully weathered her own difficulties, she counseled, "Kids are remarkably resilient, even at a young age."

Dan spoke with the authority of a father of four. "They are also curious. Landry would have been asking these questions eventually, and putting two and two together. Best you go ahead and deal with it now and get it out of the way."

Everyone, Brooke noted, seemed to be in agreement with Nate. Except her.

"At least you've got time to prepare for whatever the results are," Travis said.

"Which is why—in the meantime—I want to do everything I can to get Landry moved into the main house, with me." Nate paused and looked straight at Brooke. "I want us to be a family in every sense before the results come in."

Chapter Eight

"This is going to be a computer room slash media center where we'll have everything you need to read, study and do homework," Nate told the boys after dinner the following day, as they toured a large, second-floor space in the mansion. "And next to it is going to be a video gaming room, where you can hang out and entertain friends."

Brooke noted that Cole smiled with all the enthusiasm Nate could have wished for—even though technically none of this was meant for her son, since he wouldn't be living here much longer.

"Sweet," Cole said.

Being careful not to touch the freshly painted walls, Landry stood with his hands stuffed in the pockets of his camp shorts, as usual. He had been remote and moody like this ever since the DNA tests were done.

Brooke and Nate had concurred it was best to give Landry his space for the first twenty-four hours. Now, they were beginning to worry. Hence Nate's rush to somehow get Landry involved in the design of his new home.

Nate continued down the hall to the next set of rooms, a bedroom and private bath suite. He looked at Landry. "What do you think about this for your bedroom?"

To Brooke's and Nate's frustration, there was no response either way.

"You can have whatever you want in here—just let Brooke know," Nate persisted.

"I'd be happy to help you pick out furniture and linens in whatever colors and styles you like," she offered amiably.

The positive attitude toward the future that Brooke knew Nate had hoped to see was nowhere in sight. Landry remained emotionally and physically aloof. He stepped away from the group, the look in his eyes far too cynical for his years. "Thanks for the offer, Nate, but—"

Uh-oh, Brooke thought, *here it comes....*

"—it's enough right now for me to sleep in the caretaker's cottage," Landry continued. "You've been really great, especially under the circumstances, but you don't need to do anything more. Especially since I might not be staying."

Nate tensed, and Brooke caught the flash of hurt on his face. Her heart went out to him, even as he recovered his composure.

"I thought we had settled that, Landry," he said.

"Until the DNA results come in—" Landry scowled with the might of all fourteen of his years "—nothing is settled." He turned to Cole, done with the revitalization tour of the mansion, and Nate's cheerful efforts to turn it into a more kid-friendly environment. "Want to go for a swim?"

Cole nodded, as if eager to get away from the animosity that had been simmering just below the surface for almost two days now. "Sure."

The two boys sauntered off in wary silence.

Nate and Brooke remained in the upstairs hallway. "Go ahead and say it," he said.

She looked at him, a question in her eyes.

"You think I'm being a little too pushy."

Well, duh, yes, of course. Avoiding the wet paint, Brooke started down the sweeping front staircase. She paused, her hand on the railing, and waited for Nate to catch up with her.

Like her, he was still in his work clothes, although he had taken off his suit coat and tie. And later unfastened the first two buttons on his shirt and rolled up his sleeves.

The sense of added formality helped—until Brooke found her gaze riveted on the strong column of his throat, and the dark hair springing out the open V on his starched shirt.

Curtailing the urge to explore both, she turned her gaze to the handsome planes of his face. Realizing she could spend all day—and all night—just looking at him, she chided wryly, "What happened to the plan to let Landry take his time, deciding this was where he wanted to be, before forging on with the details?"

Nate made a face—guilty as charged.

He sat down on the stairs, clasped her elbow and brought her down beside him. "I want Landry to realize I'm serious about adopting him, and plan to go ahead with it no matter what the DNA test reveals."

Once again, without warning, they were involved in an intimate conversation. Once again she felt her heart going out to him. Even if his actions were wrong, she knew his motivation came from the right place.

She watched him stretch his long legs over several stairs.

Wanting to be more comfortable, she did the same. "I admire your determination."

It was all she could do not to reach over and grip his hand.

Keeping his own hands to himself, he turned his head and met her gaze. "I hear an 'exception' in there," he noted, with a quiet smile that also indicated he wasn't about to change his mind.

Brooke brushed the hair out of her eyes and tried anyway. "I also know what it's like to be part of a family where decisions are made for you, your input disregarded." She paused to let her words sink in, and continued searching his face. "It's not a great way to live, Nate."

He turned slightly, so his spine was pressed against the railing, his bent knee pressed against her thigh. "Are we talking about your life with your parents?"

Aware of the steady warmth emanating between them, Brooke shook her head. Heart racing, she kept her gaze locked with his. "While I still had them, my folks were great. I'm speaking of my late husband." Wanting Nate to understand, she forced herself to talk about what she had always kept to herself, for fear of feeling disloyal. "It's what happens when you marry someone twenty years older than you, who thinks he has all the answers and you have none."

The understanding in Nate's expression encouraged her to go on confiding in him. And this time she did reach over and clasp his hand, tightening her fingers around his. "The only difference was, in my case, I believed Seamus was the sole authority on everything for a very long time. And that in turn led me to doubt everything I thought I knew about myself." Brooke paused. With effort, she withdrew her hand and stood. "I know you are used to running a corporation, that you built your business on your own. But you can't behave the same way in your relationship with Landry and expect him to want to be your son."

"Do you want the bad news first or the good news?" Brooke asked Nate the following morning, after she had dropped the boys at computer camp and returned to the mansion.

Nate, who'd been about to leave for work himself, set his briefcase beside the front door. "The good."

"Both the boys are really excited about your plans for the rooms upstairs."

"That's great." Nate had been up half the night researching the latest electronic equipment, games and educational software for college-bound teens. "What's the bad?" He moved back to allow the construction crew to enter.

Brooke waited until the men walked past before she continued in a low, worried tone. "Landry told Cole that he had been thinking about running away before his great-grandmother left him with you. He said he probably would have done so had Cole and I not showed up and allowed him to stay with us in the cottage. As long as we're here, Landry plans to stick around, but he won't guarantee anything once we leave."

"Angling to stay on?" Nate teased.

Brooke rolled her eyes. "Uh—no." She sobered. "Cole is really concerned about Landry taking off. And so am I. We don't want to see anything happen to him."

"Nor do I." Nate exhaled.

"Anyway, I thought you should know."

"Thanks for giving me the heads-up." He paused. "Although for the record, I think it's just talk. If Landry was going to bolt, he would have already done so. In any case, I don't think he would go very far from his great-grandmother."

"Have you talked to him about going to see Jessalyn at her new quarters?"

"Twice. He's resistant." Nate sighed. "I'm hopeful if I keep asking every few days, he'll eventually change his mind."

"Me, too. I think it would help."

"Speaking of help… I don't know if I have articulated how grateful I am for all your help with Landry."

"You're paying me double time. That's thanks enough."

"Brooke—"

Her phone rang.

She checked the caller ID and frowned. "Do you mind if I get this? It's Percy Dearborn, the intellectual-property lawyer."

Nate gestured for her to do so, then walked off to the side to wait. When she had finished her conversation, Brooke ended the call.

Nate came back. "Everything okay?"

She only wished. "Apparently, the proof Iris Lomax is offering is flimsy at best. But the attorney wants me to go through Seamus's papers. See if I can find anything that will establish the work was definitely his. Otherwise, she's going to go ahead and file a lawsuit, and it will become public."

"Is it possible it's a scam?"

Brooke considered for a moment. "It could be. Or maybe she's just angry because he died in her arms and left her without anything, not even a mention in his will, and she finally sees a way to garner some inheritance for herself. It's hard to tell. All I really know is that this has to be done right away, so I'm going to have to ask you for the rest of the day off."

"You've got it. And Brooke—good luck."

"HEY, NATE, IT'S COLE. I'm sorry to bother you at the office, but, uh…Landry and I are in kind of a jam."

Please tell me you haven't done something stupid like try and run away, Nate thought, immediately wishing he had taken Brooke's warning more seriously.

Calmly, he stepped out of the meeting with his top managers, taking his cell phone down the hall to his private office. Resisting the parental urge to immediately start with the third degree, he asked matter-of-factly, "What can I do to help?"

"Well...Landry and I both forgot to get our permission slips signed for the field trip this afternoon."

Nate paused. "What field trip?"

"I guess we forgot to tell you. The camp is taking anyone who wants to go to a motion capture and virtual reality lab for kids at the University of Texas at Dallas this afternoon. And then out for pizza and a movie this evening. Only we can't go unless we have written permission, and I can't get ahold of Mom for some reason." Anxiety filled his voice. "And you can't sign for me, only Landry—I already asked. But you can fax in the permission slip. So if I can fax that to you, and you sign it and fax it right back, then Landry can go. But I can't unless we can find Mom before one o'clock." Cole heaved a big sigh.

"Let me give you my private fax number. Of course I'll sign."

"What about Mom?" Cole sounded glum.

She's at your house, going through boxes of your father's things, Nate thought. However, he knew revealing that would invite questions neither he nor Brooke were prepared to answer. "I'll track her down and take a copy of the permission slip over to her, and we'll get it faxed back in for you, too," Nate promised.

"Are you sure you have time?" Cole asked, sounding excited and upbeat again.

Nate looked at his watch; it was eleven-thirty. This part of parenting he could handle, no problem. "Positive. One way or another, Cole, I'll make sure you and Landry both get to go."

"Thanks, Nate." Cole's happiness was a palpable thing. "I knew we could count on you."

Nate smiled. Now, if only Landry felt the same way, they'd be all set.

BROOKE WAS IN THE MIDDLE of the living-room floor, surrounded by boxes and piles of papers and notebooks when the doorbell rang. She was half tempted not to answer it, but a glance out the window had her leaping to her feet.

Sure something was really wrong, since Nate was here unexpectedly, she headed for the door. "What's going on?" She took in his harried look and ushered him in.

"Sorry to interrupt. I've got some papers that need signing ASAP." Briefly, he explained.

Relieved it was only a paperwork snafu, Brooke relaxed.

"So if you have a fax…?" Nate smiled.

"Actually, I do." She paused to read the sheet, fill in the pertinent data and lifted a staying hand. "Let me go send these in and then I'll be right back."

Nate nodded.

Brooke disappeared down the hallway of her century-old bungalow.

While the beeps of a fax number being typed in sounded in the distance, Nate took a moment to look around.

Located in the residential enclave next to the Fort Worth university where her husband had taught, the house had both historic charm and modern appeal. It was cozy and stylish, warm and inviting—a lot like Brooke.

She returned, still clad in the trim lavender cotton skirt and sleeveless white blouse she'd had on earlier. But the panty hose and fancy sandals were gone. Barefoot and bare-legged, with her silky hair falling loosely around her shoulders, she looked gorgeous and slightly frazzled. The latter made him want to assist her all the more. "I phoned the camp office, just to make sure, and they're all set," Brooke reported with an efficient smile. "We pick them up there at eleven forty-five this evening."

Wishing he'd thought to call ahead and invite her to lunch, Nate lingered. "I can do that, if you like."

"Actually—" Brooke clapped a weary hand to the graceful slope of her neck "—I'd appreciate it."

Thinking there still might be a way for him to help, Nate nodded toward the stacks of materials. "Any luck with the search?"

Brooke's face fell. "Yes and no. I didn't find the proof I was looking for, but I did find this." She handed over a sheaf of papers bound together with elastic.

Their fingers brushed as the exchange was made.

On top was a cover letter from the publisher of Seamus's new volume of poetry. Nate noted the date. "This was sent three years ago."

"In response to another proposed manuscript," Brooke affirmed, looking all the more distressed.

Nate read aloud, "'Dear Seamus… It is with regret I inform you that The Poet's Press can not publish your new collection. The poems are much too dark and cynical. We want more works that capture the wonder and magic of falling in love again, not a detailed exposition of what it is to fall out of love and feel trapped in a marriage one regrets. We fear this collection would alienate the readers of your first three volumes, and damage sales of future works, as well. We advise you to go back to the themes that made your earlier works a success, and of course, we would like a first look at them when they are ready to be read….'"

Nate looked beneath the letter, at the manuscript. "Did you know about this?"

Brooke shook her head.

His concern for her well-being deepened. "Did you read any of this?"

She nodded. And then, without warning, burst into tears. Embarrassed, she tried to hide her face and move away.

Nate did the only thing he could—he pulled her into a hug. "Hey," he said, smoothing her hair with the flat of his hand. "It's okay."

"No." Her voice was muffled against his shoulder. "It's not. Nate, my husband loathed being married to me. He compared me to an anchor weighing him down, keeping him trapped in a sea of mediocrity."

"I'm sure it was an exaggeration. Poetic license…"

Brooke had lied to herself for years. Tried to give her late husband the benefit of the doubt. The poems she had read, the raw emotion in them, had opened her eyes. Wanting Nate to understand, she swallowed and explained, "For years I felt like a burden to Seamus. As if Cole and I were in the way." She shook her head in misery as the memories of unhappier times came flooding back. "I told myself it was because Seamus was an artist, and he was blocked— that he needed more time for his art…fewer demands from us… And I tried to give him that. But the reality is he never loved me. Never cared about me, the person."

The way I feel you caring about me…

Nate took her face in his palms. "That's impossible."

"No, it isn't. Nate…"

He smoothed a hand through her hair. "Listen to me, Brooke. You are one of the most lovable women I have ever met." He kissed her temple, then drew back, desire in his eyes. "You're beautiful and smart and amazing. If your husband didn't see that—" Nate rubbed the pad of his thumb across her lower lip "—then he was a fool." He flattened a hand against her spine and brought her closer still. "But I see it." He shifted her so her back was against the wall, his tall body pressed against hers.

Brooke struggled to keep her feelings in check, but it was an impossible task when he was holding her flush against him. The pandemonium inside her multiplied as he moved closer still, his sinewy chest molding to the softness of her breasts. Her skin registered the heat, and the hardness of his body compared to hers.

Nate flashed a slow, sexy smile as his head slanted slowly and deliberately over hers. "Wow, do I see it."

This time there was nothing tentative about his kiss. It was hot, persuasive, hungry. He was holding her tightly and it still wasn't enough. She wanted more of the slow, demanding caress of his lips, the feel of his hands sliding up and down her back. She wanted more of his kindness and understanding, and the womanly way he made her feel. She wanted to let go of the hurt and disappointment of the past, and live in the moment. And Nate seemed only too eager to comply.

As she encircled her arms about his neck and melted against him, she could feel the pounding of his heart matching hers, and the strength and power of his need. Once again they were completely caught up in the passionate tangling of their lips and tongues. And this time she made no attempt to put on the brakes. It had been two long years since she had been touched. Never before had she felt so cherished. Nate made her feel like living life to the ultimate. He made her want to take the risk. And though initially Brooke had feared he was as self-possessed and driven as her late husband, that despite his ease with people, he was too emotionally aloof to give and receive love, she realized she'd judged him unfairly. And as Nate continued to kiss and hold her, she realized he wasn't just prone to doing the honorable thing in whatever situation he found himself, he was a generous and affectionate man.

Kind enough to bring her out of her self-imposed chastity and back into a balanced life, where she had her son and her work—and mind-blowing passion....

Even if it was destined to be only a brief, impulsive affair.

Brooke knew she could handle it. Because she was still in full control of her emotions and knew exactly what this was.

She wouldn't make the mistake she had made before, confusing her need for comfort and support with falling in love.

She and Nate were friends who needed a little help getting through two unexpected personal crises—that was all. When their situations returned to normal, so would their lives....

Undoubtedly, Nate would go his merry way, she would go hers. With a memory of one hot-blooded lovemaking session going with them... But in the meantime, she intended to enjoy every second of pleasure and relief he had to offer.

NATE HADN'T PLANNED to take Brooke in his arms today. He had expected to come over, get her signature, see how things were going and be on his way. But remaining detached from her was proving impossible. He couldn't be with her and not want her. Not just as a parenting mentor or friend, but as a woman. His woman. And his need for exclusivity stunned him. He hadn't felt this intensely about a woman in...well, ever. And that fueled even more his need to possess her. He wanted to take her to bed and make wild passionate love to her, so thoroughly and completely they'd both remember it forever.

"The question is," he murmured as she kissed him back, moaning softly as his hands came around to slide sensuously over her breasts. He kissed her cheek, her temple, the shell of her ear, before returning ever so slowly to her lips. "Do *you* see how sexy you are?"

He dropped his hand down, pushing her skirt higher, to caress the insides of her thighs. Just that had her trembling with pleasure. "I'm beginning to," she murmured, between subsequent kisses.

"Good." He slid a hand beneath her knees and her back and lifted her in his arms. Headed in the direction of her bedroom and deposited her gently next to her four-poster bed. As her bare feet hit the carpet, he told her, "Because we're just getting started."

Brooke chuckled softly and slid her deliciously full lower lip out into a seductive pout. Splaying her hands across his chest, she gave him a look that let him know this afternoon was strictly for fun, nothing more. "Promises, promises…"

It sounded like a dare. Nate toed off his shoes, stripped off his shirt and pants. "Nothing I like more than a challenge," he murmured.

Nothing she liked more, he noticed as he stripped completely, than turning him on.

Her eyes widened at the proof of his desire. "Wow," she said.

Wow was right, Nate thought. He'd never been this aroused. "My turn." He planted one hand at the nape of her neck, the other at the base of her spine. Hauling her close, he dipped his head. Reveling in her soft gasp of desire, he delivered a long, soul-searching kiss. Her response was immediate. She swept her tongue into his mouth and brought him closer still. Nate drank in the sweet taste of her, luxuriating in the lilac fragrance of her hair and skin.

She groaned again as his hands moved beneath the hem of her blouse to her breasts. He cupped the full, soft weight through the lace of her bra. "Not fair," she murmured with an impatient sigh, "that I'm the only one still dressed...."

With her hair tumbling over her shoulders, her cheeks flushed, her lips damp and parted, she had never looked more beautiful. Or vulnerable. Nate's need to protect her expanded. "We can rectify that," he whispered, satisfaction roaring in his veins.

Seeing no need to rush through one of the most memorable days of his life, he took his time as he unbuttoned, unclasped and unzipped. He liked the way Brooke's chest rose and fell with each ragged intake of breath, the way she couldn't seem to take her eyes off him, any more than he could take his off her.

She trembled as he divested her of bra and bikini underwear, then bent and kissed her budding pink nipples, one by one. She clasped his shoulders and sighed contentedly as his mouth moved urgently over her soft curves.

He dropped to his knees, kissing the hollow of her stomach, stroking the insides of her soft thighs. He traced her navel with his tongue, then dropped lower still, to administer the most ardent of kisses. Overcome with pleasure, shuddering with sensation, she whispered, "Nate..."

She shifted position and her lips drifted over his skin, touching, exploring, until there was no more control, no more hesitation, and Nate drew her to the bed. Feeling how much Brooke wanted and needed him, he lay down with her on the lace-edged sheets. His own body throbbing, he used a light caress to convince her to part her legs for him again. Her head fell back as he found the sweet sensitive spot with the pad of his thumb, until she was rocking slightly, leaving no doubt about what they both needed to have.

Watching her face, and trembling with a depth of feeling he could no longer deny, Nate guided her legs around his waist. Savoring the intimacy and the wonder of it all, he plunged into her and began to thrust. Her body closed around him and cloaked him in warmth. What few boundaries existed between them evaporated. Amazingly, fittingly, they were one. As he took them to the limit and beyond, he knew in his heart nothing had ever felt so right.

BROOKE HAD NO SOONER come back down to earth than the guilt and uncertainty set in. She had never acted so selfishly in her life, prior to this. And as much as she wanted to romanticize what had just happened between her and Nate, she knew she had just made love with him for all the wrong reasons. As a salve to her bruised ego, and her even more wounded heart... The last thing she had wanted to do was hurt Nate. Or herself.

Reluctantly, she extricated herself from his warm and tender embrace, and sat up against the headboard. "I can't believe I just did that."

He rolled to his side, a paragon of rippling muscles and masculine satisfaction. Looking as if he wanted nothing more than to make her his all over again, he queried contentedly, "Made love on impulse in the middle of the afternoon?"

Brooke knew if she let him he would shatter whatever caution she had left. And she had too much responsibility to allow that to happen. Her pulse racing, she held the sheet to her breasts with one hand and pushed her hair away from her face with the other. For both their sakes, she had to be honest and let him know where they stood. He could deal with it.

She sighed and looked deep into his eyes with self-effacing candor. "I used you to make myself feel better."

Chapter Nine

For a second, Nate couldn't believe he had heard right. "You didn't use me," he said. "Any more than I used you. We came together because it was what we wanted."

Brooke rose, blanket wrapped around her, and went to her closet. When she emerged, she had on a calf-length terry robe. She looked beautiful and disheveled, and very much on edge. "Be that as it may," she told him softly, "I don't want us to do this again."

Determined to keep this from going south, Nate leveled his gaze on her and forced her to be specific. "You don't want us to spend time alone together?" Which had been great. "Get closer?" A feat that had been even more satisfying. He rose from the bed, slid on his shorts, then his slacks. "Make love?"

He knew from the darkening of her irises that he'd hit the mark.

Brooke lifted her chin, defiant. Her fingers tightened on the fabric of her robe. "I don't want our friendship—" She paused, fumbling with a hairbrush "—if that's what it is—"

"It is."

"—to morph into a romantic love that we both know will never last."

Nate watched, fascinated, as she restored order to her

silky hair. The pressure against his fly told him his desire for her wasn't going away anytime soon. And he knew the feeling was mutual. "And if our chemistry does last?" he interjected. "Then what?" What excuse would she use to run away from the best thing *he'd* ever felt, anyway?

Brooke perched on the edge of her bed. She dropped her brush into her lap, took his hand and drew him down beside her so they were sitting face-to-face. The contrite expression on her face told him she thought she had hurt his feelings. "Listen to me, Nate," she murmured. "You and I are together now because of the work I am doing for you, and because you need help bringing Landry all the way into your life."

Nate wouldn't deny that Brooke had filled his life with gentle understanding, tenderness and contentment, any more than he could deny the soft warmth of her fingers over his, or the fact she was the best thing to ever come into his life, hands down. "It's more than that," he argued gruffly. Without even trying, she understood what he needed and wanted. He'd *thought* he comprehended what she longed for in her life, too.

Her ambivalent expression said otherwise.

She swallowed, seemingly as reluctant to dis him as she was to make love with him again. "You're right," Brooke agreed. "My world has been turned upside down and I need the distraction, too. Heck—" she grinned crookedly "—I needed the ego boost. But once we get past these twin crises, our lives will return to normal, and we won't need each other anymore."

The hell they wouldn't, Nate thought, already aware of how lonely and empty his life would be without her and her son. And it wasn't just him. Landry would be devastated, too.

Brooke wet her lower lip. "And when we no longer need each other, we'll go our separate ways."

Nate tore his eyes from the soft curves of her breasts, visible in the V-neckline of her robe. "You're assuming a lot," he told her quietly.

Sadness crept into her eyes. "And with good reason, Nate. I've done this before. When I was a senior in college and my life was filled with uncertainty, I reached out to a man who seemed to have all the answers."

Seamus. Her lying, cheating, selfish jerk of a husband.

"I confused the friendship and the physical passion—and an even more pressing need for a complete family of my own again—with the kind of love that would last a lifetime. It didn't."

"But that doesn't mean what we are feeling—whatever this is—won't," Nate countered.

"Which is exactly the problem," Brooke argued, a vulnerable sheen in her eyes. "We don't really know what this is. All I know for certain is that had I not been in distress today…had you not shown up when you did…I wouldn't have reached out to you. We wouldn't have recklessly fallen into bed and made love. Because I don't do things like this, Nate." Her voice rose emphatically. "I don't have flings or affairs. For me, making love is a commitment." She swallowed, still holding his gaze. "Or it should be."

"I agree," Nate said. "And for the record, I don't sleep around, either."

Brooke shrugged, let go of his hand and stood. "Then we're on the same page."

Yes, Nate thought. *And no.* The time he had spent with Brooke and the boys had shown him everything he had been missing, not having a wife and children of his own. Maybe it was selfish of him to not want to let go of the makeshift family they had formed in the last week. He didn't care. He didn't want to give that up any more than he wanted to give her up. "I readily admit we jumped the gun a bit today, but what we just experienced was more than pure physical passion, or wrongheaded crisis management," he said.

She grinned at his subtle joke, but to his disappointment kept her defenses firmly in place. "How do you know?"

Because passion alone left you wanting to run the other way when your needs were met. Something more had you wanting to stay. This was something more, Nate thought. But not sure Brooke would accept his revelation as anything more than some cheesy line—the kind her late "love poet" husband had apparently been full of—Nate stuck to the facts.

"I won't stop wanting you," he told her firmly.

Her expression clouded. "If you did, it wouldn't be the first time it's happened to me," she said bitterly.

And once again Nate found himself paying for the sins of Seamus Mitchell.

"The point is—" Brooke picked up his discarded shirt and handed it to him "—it's not a position I want to put myself in. Not again. I like you, Nate. I do."

Wasn't that what Seraphina had said when they broke up? Nate wondered, shrugging on his shirt, then pulling on his socks and shoes.

"I want us to be friends," Brooke said, her expression determined, as she showed him to the door. "But friends and confidants are all we can be."

"YOU WANT TO TELL US WHAT the problem is?" Dan drawled at five o'clock Friday evening, as Nate, Travis and Dan gathered in the large mansion kitchen. "Or just leave us to guess?"

In no mood to play games, Nate demanded impatiently, "What are you talking about?"

Travis lifted a brow. "Well, either you don't like what Dan's architect and my company's construction crews have done to your kitchen, or you've got a problem elsewhere. And judging by Landry's and Cole's delight at the array of computer and electronic equipment that was just delivered and carted up to the second floor just now, it's not with either of the boys."

"They are happy," Nate acknowledged. At least for the moment, he added mentally. That too could change on a dime. "And the kitchen is great." Thanks to Brooke's collaboration with the guys, it no longer looked like a caterer's prep space, but a place where a family could hang out and cook together. The only problem was, the only woman he could envision there was not interested in being around long term....

"Then what is it?" Dan persisted. He exchanged knowing glances with Travis. "Or should we just say who...?"

Nate did not normally discuss his problems with women. However, these weren't the usual circumstances.

He walked over to the window—made sure Brooke was still outside talking to the furniture company guys, who had just delivered a whole houseful of new furniture—then walked back to his friends and admitted, "It's Brooke. I'm interested, but she just wants to be 'friends.'"

Dan and Travis both winced, easily understanding his pain.

"No chemistry on her part, huh?" Travis guessed.

Nate would understand, if that had been the case.

"Then you have to keep trying," Dan said. "Let her know you're serious."

"Build on the friendship and go from there," Travis advised. "It's what I did with Holly when we were ready for more."

And it had worked, Nate recalled. Holly and Travis were

spectacularly happy now, as were the rest of his married friends.

"Although you might want to delay the real pursuit until her work for you is done," Dan said.

"You didn't," Nate pointed out. Dan had fallen in love with Emily and proposed to her while she was still working as a personal chef for him and his kids....

"Not waiting made it harder to establish a relationship, not easier," Dan insisted.

"I'm not averse to challenge," Nate said.

"That we know." Travis grinned. "We're just saying be careful not to let your impatience get in the way of what you really want here."

Which was Brooke, Nate thought.

And not just, as she still thought, for the short term.

"So what do you think, Mom?" Cole asked late the next afternoon. "Did we or did we not do the most awesome job ever setting up the computer and game rooms?"

"You guys did a fantastic job," Brooke agreed, taking the tour of the two spaces with Cole and Landry. Her touches included the comfortable sectional sofas, shelving systems and computer workstations; Nate and the boys had selected and put together all the electronics. The end result was a state-of-the-art study and social space, decorated in hardy fabrics and bright, teen-friendly colors.

"You are so lucky," Cole told Landry. He looked around with an admiring glance. "I only wish I could have a setup like this in our house. But my dad would never even let me have a video game system."

Out of the corner of her eye, Brooke saw Nate work to keep his own expression inscrutable. Embarrassed, she told her son, "I didn't know you wanted one." Cole had always acted as if Wii and PlayStation were for other kids.

He shrugged. "I figured you felt the same way as Dad did."

She hadn't. "I wish I'd known how you felt."

"You never disagreed with him on that kind of stuff. So it would have been pointless to ask."

Guilt hit hard. What else had Cole been afraid to talk to her about? "We can get one now," Brooke promised. "When we go back home." The live-in bonus she was getting on this job would pay for that and much more.

Cole grinned. "Way cool, Mom."

"No problem." Avoiding the concern she saw in Nate's eyes, Brooke flashed a smile. "About dinner…"

"Uh…" Cole looked at Landry.

Landry took over. "We were hoping we could invite some of our friends from computer camp to come over tonight and check it out."

"Maybe have some pizza," Cole added.

Brooke glanced at Nate. Although he hadn't said as much, she sensed he had been hoping for a quiet "family night." But when he took in the happy, hopeful faces of the kids, he shrugged and said, "Sounds good to me. Start making the calls."

By 8:00 p.m., they had ten boys gathered upstairs. Nate, who had been busy assisting with the fine-tuning of the game and computer setups, finally came down to the kitchen.

Despite the fact that he had been working with the boys for eleven hours straight, getting everything just the way they wanted it, Brooke thought Nate had never looked happier or more content.

He was such a *dad*.

Cole was right—Landry was indeed one lucky kid.

She was the one who was unlucky. Falling for the wrong

guy at the right time, then the right guy at the wrong time...

She knew Nate had been surprised by her emotional withdrawal the day before, but what choice had she had? Their decisions could affect two kids. They couldn't afford to be rash. As much as she wanted to, she couldn't take advantage of Nate's temporary vulnerability by letting him think he could only be a good father to Landry if she were in the picture, too. Because it just wasn't so. Nate and Landry would be fine, given a little time. Nate was a natural when it came to parenthood, even if he didn't quite see that yet.

And she couldn't let herself turn to him to help find her way out of the darkness she temporarily found herself in. Because the truth was, the situation with Iris Lomax and Seamus's publisher would get resolved. And once this crisis passed, she and Cole would be fine, too.

In the meantime, it didn't matter how tempted she was. It would be a mistake to lean on Nate, the way she had once leaned on her husband. She could get through this situation on her own. The last two years of widowhood had shown her that.

She needed to follow Nate's lead and pretend that their lovemaking had never happened. Even if doing so left her feeling more alone than she had ever imagined.

Brooke turned her attention back to the task at hand. "How is the food holding out up there?"

Nate lounged against the counter. "All the snacks you set out are pretty much gone. Same with the soft drinks."

As she passed by him, she was inundated with his brisk male scent. "The pizza should be here any minute."

"I'm sure they'll devour that, too." He watched her unwrap a stack of paper plates and set them on the counter, next to the napkins and ice-filled paper cups. "Listen,

I hope I didn't cause a problem for you—regarding the video-game system."

Brooke held up a hand. "I meant what I said up there. I do intend to get Cole one as soon as possible."

Nate nodded, his expression impassive.

Brooke felt compelled to explain, "I just didn't realize he had ever asked Seamus for one."

Nate's brow furrowed. "Your husband wouldn't have mentioned it to you?"

She shrugged self-consciously. "I doubt he felt it was worth his time. He wasn't interested in any nonintellectual pursuits. And he had no patience for doing anything with children of any age."

"I was under the impression he wanted a child when you married."

Comforted by Nate's steady male presence, Brooke explained, "It was more of an ego thing. Which isn't to say Seamus wasn't enormously proud of his son—he was. He made sure he took Cole to many a public event and introduced him around, which Cole loved. Seamus just never spent quality time with Cole, the way you have the past week."

Which was yet another reason why she was attracted to Nate.

It wasn't just his kindness and understanding attitude, it was his knack for integrating others into his life, even his capacity for love….

Whoever ended up living happily-ever-after with Nate was going to be one lucky woman….

"It's been my pleasure to get to know Cole," Nate continued sincerely. "You know that."

His voice sent ripples of desire up and down her spine. "I do."

Silence stretched between them.

She could feel his pull as strongly as the earth's gravity. Brooke swallowed, aware she was seconds from reaching out for him, telling him her decision to rebuff him had been a terrible mistake. "Nate…"

Footsteps sounded on the stairs. Seconds later, Cole came bursting into the room, joy radiating from every inch of him. He sprinted to Nate's side and wrapped his arms around him. "Nate! You gotta come upstairs and see this! Please!"

Nate returned Cole's brief, impromptu hug and ear-to-ear grin. Oblivious to Brooke's concern, he slung his arm around Cole's shoulders and off they went.

BROOKE MANAGED TO KEEP her distance from Nate the rest of the evening. It wasn't hard. Shortly after Cole had come down to get him, Landry had trotted down to retrieve her. Brooke had spent the remainder of the night alternately observing and officiating the teen tournament. When she wasn't doing that, she was replenishing the food and beverage tables—a feat that sounded easier than it had been, as all of them seemed to have huge appetites and stomachs that were bottomless pits.

Finally, at eleven-thirty, the last of the parents arrived to pick up their sons. Nate helped Cole and Landry restore order to the upstairs rooms, while Brooke went downstairs to work on the kitchen.

Finished, the boys appeared there. Nate trailed after them.

"Need help, Mom?" Cole asked.

Brooke looked at their faces. The excitement of the day had finally caught up with them. Both teens looked ready to collapse. "Why don't you guys head back to the cottage and hit the sack?"

Landry squinted at her, seeming to realize the kitchen

was another fifteen minutes or more from being squared away. "You sure?" he asked around a yawn.

Brooke nodded. She stepped between the boys, caught their shoulders and gave them each an affectionate squeeze. "Positive. Now go. Before you fall asleep on your feet and I have to carry you both to bed!"

Cole and Landry chuckled, but didn't argue. They seemed to finally realize how tired they were.

The boys departed.

Suddenly, it was just Nate and Brooke. "Surely there's something I can do," he said.

The idea of working side by side with him was appealing. Too appealing. Her pulse skittering as she thought about kissing him again, she turned away from his ruggedly sexy frame. "Thanks, but I can handle it." She had to get a grip here. Stop fantasizing and pretending life was simpler than it was.

She went back to loading serving platters in the dishwasher. "You can go—" She stopped just short of saying *Go on to bed.* And wary of the implications of that, swiftly amended it to a lame, "do...whatever...."

"Mmm-hmm."

There was a wealth of meaning in that presumptuous sound.

Perspiration broke out on the back of her neck, between her thighs, behind her knees, in the valley between her breasts.

Nate edged closer. He was standing behind her, so near she could feel the warmth of his breath on the top of her head.

Another ribbon of desire swept through her.

He waited.

Her head down, she kept busy cleaning.

"Why do I think I did something wrong?"

Brooke had to stand on tiptoe and reach across the counter to get the last platter. "I don't know what you mean."

When her fingers fell short of it, he leaned over, grasped it for her and set it in the sink.

Before she could pick it up, his fingers closed gently over her wrist, stilling the restless movement. "Stop cleaning for a minute," he urged softly, "and just talk to me."

Brooke forced herself to turn toward him. "My son looks at you with such hero worship in his eyes."

Nate acknowledged this with a modest dip of her head. "And that's a problem because...what? I'm not a hero?" he prodded drily.

That was the problem, he *was!*

And not just to the boys.

Telling herself she was not going to make the same mistake twice, Brooke frowned. "What's going to happen to Cole when this job ends, as it will in another week, and he doesn't see you anymore?"

Nate looked affronted. "He'll see me."

Brooke fought the urge to tear out her hair in frustration. "You know what I mean," she insisted.

"You're right," Nate said grimly. "It won't be the same."

So it wasn't just her, Brooke thought victoriously. Nate was thinking ahead, anticipating the difficulties and pitfalls, too.

Emboldened, she continued, "Landry's like a brother to him."

"And vice versa," Nate agreed.

"And that's great. But what happens if something damages their friendship or ours?"

Nate's lips thinned in obvious irritation. "It won't," he stated plainly.

"But if it does," she insisted.

He let out a long breath. "You're borrowing trouble."

Feeling on the verge of an emotion she couldn't control, Brooke moved away, grabbing the spray bottle of granite cleaner and a cloth. Aware of the way Nate was suddenly studying her, sizing her up, perhaps plotting his next move, she babbled nervously, "Which is funny, really, because I never see trouble coming. I always get blindsided."

Her parents' demise, her husband's infidelity and resultant death, the plagiarism claim…all had come with no warning.

Now she was seeing danger around every corner….

It was ironic, really. How much she wanted to take the risk and be with Nate. And how terribly, deeply afraid she was of doing just that.

If only she could be sure…. If only love came with guarantees.

But it didn't.

And she couldn't let her heart be stolen and smashed into pieces again.

Nate held out his arms to her. "Brooke…"

Tears of disappointment blurring her eyes, she rushed past him. "I can't, Nate! I can't…."

He closed the distance between them in two long strides and wrapped his arms around her. "You can take it one day—one moment—at a time," he whispered, holding her close, making her want to believe it was so. "We both will. It's the only choice we have."

Chapter Ten

Nate hadn't kissed her—hadn't even tried. So why was she feeling so let down? This was what she had wanted. Yet…being separated from him this way felt wrong, too, Brooke realized as she returned to the caretaker's cottage and went on to bed.

She slept fitfully. And dreamed of Nate over and over again. Which was why, when the guys brought up the amusement park idea early the next morning, she found herself forgoing work and accompanying them and Nate.

Naturally, no sooner had they walked through the gates than all three males headed straight for the scariest roller coaster. Billed as the tallest, fastest coaster in the Southwest, it was twenty-four stories tall and accelerated from 0 to 70 in four seconds. Just looking at it made Brooke feel ill.

"Come on, Mom, you can do it!" Cole tugged on her hand and urged her in the direction he wanted her to go.

"Look at the way you're latched in." Landry pointed to the sturdy over-the-shoulder-and-chest contraption that kept riders in place even when they were zooming through the loops upside down.

Nate caught Brooke's eye. He seemed to know her dilemma. She wanted to share in the fun with the rest of them, yet she was completely terrified. Prior to this, she had declared Cole not old enough for the most thrilling rides in the park. Now, given the way he'd grown in the last year, and the fact that he more than topped the height requirement for the ride, she had no such excuse.

"You'll be perfectly safe," Landry assured her.

Cole regarded her with hopeful eyes. "Please, Mom, don't let us down! Say yes!"

Brooke thought about all the similar experiences Cole had been denied over the years, because Seamus had not deemed them worthy of his time.

All her son wanted was to be a kid. Forget he'd lost a father. And enjoy the fact he'd found a spiritual "brother" in Landry, and a "surrogate dad" in Nate.

What was a little fear, if not to be conquered? If she was honest, she could use a little distraction, too. She lifted a palm to high-five each of the boys. "Let's do it!"

They hooted in delight and ran to get in the line, which didn't look all that long right now, unfortunately. "Landry and I want to sit together," Cole shouted over his shoulder as they joined the queue.

Brooke nodded and lifted a hand in assent, knowing that left her to sit with Nate, since the riders went two by two on this ride.

Nate sent her a reassuring sidelong glance as they strolled through the maze of metal bars. He clapped a companionable hand on her shoulder. "It'll be over before you know it."

"Not soon enough," Brooke muttered under her breath. "My knees already feel like Jell-O."

"You're a good sport to be doing this for the guys," he said, with an approving glance that made her feel all warm and tingly inside.

"That's me," Brooke joked nervously. "Always taking one for the team…"

As was Nate…

Their glances locked, and another thrill swept through Brooke.

Before long, Cole and Landry were climbing into their seats. Seconds later, Brooke found herself sitting down, too, with Nate beside her. As soon as they were securely latched in, behind the boys, Nate reached over and took her hand. Squeezed it hard. And then they were off.

"YOU DON'T LOOK SO GOOD, Mom," Cole told Brooke what seemed like a lifetime later. In reality, only a few completely harrowing minutes had passed, minutes she had been absolutely sure she would not survive.

"Yeah," Landry noted, "you're kind of green."

She felt as if she was about to throw up.

Nate studied her with compassionate eyes. And there was no doubt about it, Brooke admitted a little resentfully, given her wuss status in the day's events thus far. Nate's own color was great. He had the same flush of exhilaration staining his face that their boys had, the same euphoric laugh as they exited the ride.

In fact, Brooke realized, surveying him closely as she tried to get her land legs back, Nate looked good all over. In sneakers, knee-length shorts and a loose fitting, short-sleeve shirt that brought out the vibrant blue of his eyes, he was the epitome of a dad on a weekend outing with the kids. Only a whole lot sexier than the other dads around them. A lot sexier, in fact, than any dad she had ever seen.

The realization brought heat to her cheeks.

Nate's brow furrowed.

Obviously, he had misinterpreted the reason behind her sudden flush.

Nate wrapped a steadying arm about her shoulders, which only made her discomfort worse. He peered at her closely before turning to Cole. "I think your mom needs to sit down a second and catch her breath." Briefly, Nate shifted his glance to the teens. "Why don't you boys ride the tower? Unless—" Nate looked back at Brooke "—you want to do that one, too?"

Just the sight of the ride had all the blood draining from her head once again. "Thirty-two and a half stories straight up and down again, at a speed of forty-five miles an hour?" Weakly, she reiterated the information in the brochure.

Cole and Landry gave each other fist bumps. "It's got the best view of the park!" Landry claimed.

Brooke lifted a hand, begging for mercy. "I don't think so," she murmured, still feeling a little shaky. "You-all go ahead and have a great time!"

"I'll stay here with your mom," Nate volunteered.

Relieved, the boys raced off to get in line.

Nate led Brooke over to an empty bench with a clear view of the ride. Propping a solicitous hand on her shoulder, he lowered his face to hers and asked with a mixture of bemusement and quiet sympathy, "Can I get you anything?"

How about a kiss? A fierce, warm hug. The opportunity to rest my head on your broad shoulder and close my eyes and forget the terror I just felt.

Knowing it couldn't happen, shocked by the notion that she was even longing for such a thing, Brooke pushed the thought away.

"How about a heart that's not pounding so hard it's about to leap out of my chest?" she quipped.

He grinned, reassured, then tapped the park map she held clutched in her hands. "We could do the less intense rides for a while."

Brooke shook her head. Cole needed her to be strong and fearless.

So she would be.

"The boys want the maximum rush today. So let's make sure they do all the fastest, highest rides at least once," she stipulated firmly.

He smiled in admiration. "You going to be able to do any more?"

"Yep." One way or another, Brooke would conquer her fear. It would be easier with the indefatigable Nate by her side. "I'm warning you, though," she teased, her good humor returning as her system settled back into a normal rhythm, "I might squeeze your hand off in the process."

"That's okay." He flashed a very sexy smile that melted her insides. "I can take it."

And take it he did, Brooke noted as the day wore on.

The park had twelve thrill rides. The boys rode them all, and Brooke managed to do ten of them, which was a personal record for her. They saw a show, ate way too much food, and even spent time playing games in the arcade before staying for the fireworks that closed down the park.

The boys talked about their adventure all the way back to Nate's.

Still reliving every adrenaline-filled moment as they all got out of Nate's car, Cole grinned. "This was the best day ever."

Landry looked Nate square in the eye and said with heartfelt sincerity, "For me, too." He hesitated before extending his hand.

Nate swallowed up Landry's palm and shook it warmly.

Aware this was the first formal physical expression of acceptance between the two, initiated by Landry, Brooke got a lump in her throat.

"Thanks, Nate," the boy said huskily.

Nate looked as if he had just won the lottery. "Anytime," he promised thickly.

His eyes suspiciously moist, Cole shook hands with Nate, too.

"It was a great day," Brooke told Nate warmly, before they said good-night.

The only thing that would have made it more perfect, she noted as she and the two teens headed for the cottage, was if the four of them had been the actual "family" they'd felt like all day.

"I'VE BEEN THINKING," Landry said the next morning, over breakfast in the newly reconfigured kitchen. "Maybe I should visit my great-grandmother, after all. I mean, she might be kind of lonely or missing me or something."

Or in other words, Brooke thought, Landry yearned to see Jessalyn now, as much as the elderly woman had been wanting to see him. "I think that's a great idea," she enthused.

"Can you take me over to the retirement village after camp today?"

Brooke set plates of blueberry oatmeal pancakes in front of each boy. She lounged against the other side of the breakfast bar. "I'll have to clear it with Nate."

"Clear what with me?" he asked, walking in.

He circled the counter to help himself to some of the coffee in the pot while Brooke explained.

"So is it okay?" Landry asked.

Nate looked longingly at the golden cakes on the griddle. "Of course. In fact, I can take you if you want."

Landry looked at Brooke, half seeming to want her to intervene, half not.

She'd never been one to manipulate a situation, but this was for the best. She plated a breakfast for Nate, too. "Actually, Landry, it would be better if Nate drove you over, schedulewise." If the two of them were alone, they'd have a chance to build on the rapport they had already established, maybe feel even more like father and son....

"Can I go, too?" Cole asked, eager to be part of things.

Everyone turned to look at him.

Nate took his breakfast and sat down on a high stool at the island counter. The closest seat available was on the other side of Cole.

"Landry?" Nate leaned forward, tossing the ball back to him.

Landry grinned at Cole with brotherly affection. "Sounds good to me...."

And there went the solo bonding time, Brooke thought with a sigh.

But maybe this was good, too.

With Cole along, Landry was less likely to back out. And he needed to visit his great-grandmother.

Because Brooke was expecting a delivery, Nate drove the boys to camp that morning, as well. Since he was already in a suit and tie, she expected him to go on to the office from there. Instead, he came back to the mansion and walked upstairs, just as the truck that had brought the furniture for Landry's bedroom in the main house was driving away.

Brooke met him in the hall. "Everything okay?"

Nate glanced at the work in progress that would one day be his son's room.

"I wanted to thank you for bringing the boys here for breakfast this morning."

Glad he hadn't thought she was overstepping, Brooke went back to unwrapping linens. "The kitchen here is much nicer now than the one in the caretaker's cottage."

"That isn't why you did it."

It had been, however, the reason she had given the boys. She climbed up the ladder and slid the covering on the mattress of the elevated loft-style bed. Digging in his heels about only being there temporarily, Landry had never committed to any one particular style or color, so Brooke had had to rely on her intuition when selecting the decor. She was confident Landry would like it, however, once he moved out of the cottage and into this room. The large suite was the perfect place for him to call home, the furniture she had selected a harbinger of college years to come, with bookshelves on one end of the loft bed's base, a built-in desk on the other. A futon and easy chair in another corner provided space for Landry to hang out while listening to music or watching TV or talking on the phone.

"Yesterday was so nice…. I thought you might like to expand on that and spend time together," she said.

Nate came in to check out the dorm-style furniture system and decor. "Which is, I'm guessing, why you wanted me to pick him up from camp today."

Brooke climbed down the ladder, unfolded a set of organic cotton sheets. "His seeing his great-grandmother again is a big deal."

Nate steadied the ladder while she climbed up to finish making the bed. "As is his taking Cole with him."

Brooke smoothed out the soft warm blanket and boldly striped duvet. "It seems like everything is finally working out the way you had hoped."

Nate handed her the pillows. "Thanks in no small part to you."

Brooke arranged them artfully, then climbed back down to stand beside Nate once again. "Don't sell yourself short, Nate. You've got a natural affinity for kids." She looked around, pleased at the way the space was coming together, then turned back to him. "You're going to be…scratch that. You *already are* a great dad."

The corner of Nate's mouth lifted as he followed her out of the bedroom. "Coming from you, that's high praise."

"It was deserved," she admitted sincerely. "Being a parent is hard but rewarding work."

"You make it look easy," he said.

Brooke flashed a tremulous smile. "And we both know it's anything but," she murmured.

"True." Suddenly, the only sound in the entire mansion was the sound of the two of them breathing.

Their glances meshed. Another second passed. Once again, Brooke had the strong sensation Nate wanted to kiss her. Almost as much as she suddenly wanted to kiss him…. And just as swiftly, she knew she had been lying to herself. "We're not going to be able to do this, are we?" she asked, knowing she could avoid this reckoning if she only had the strength to move away. But she didn't. And Nate didn't want to move away, either. He'd already made that clear.

He made it clear again as he moved toward her. "We're not going to be able to do what?"

She lifted her hands in a humorous expression of defeat. "Remain just friends."

Nate's eyes darkened. "I can be patient."

"So can I," she declared.

But as they continued looking at each other, something changed. There was a smile in Nate's eyes and they went from mutually concerned parents who had once made love and shared a great weekend together, to a man and a woman sharing something deeper, more powerful.

Brooke hadn't allowed herself to feel anything like this in a long time, and the emotions were too overwhelming to resist. She reached for Nate. "Suppose I've changed my mind." *Suppose I'm tired of being alone, tired of denying myself what I really want, which is you.* She gulped, wondering when she had gotten so bad at negotiating. As two successful businesspeople, this should be their strong point. They ought to be able to come to some meeting of the minds. "Suppose—" she paused, looking deep into his eyes "—I don't want to wait."

"The first time we made love…"

The only time.

She'd told herself she was rebounding, that it had been nothing more than a way to assuage her injured pride, to prove she was worth something as a woman again.

Brooke saw now it had been so much more, a way back into a fully lived life.

A door to the future…their future?

Or just the here and now?

She didn't know, didn't care, as long as the incredible pleasure, the intense feeling of being alive she felt whenever she was with him, didn't stop.

Nate threaded his hands through her hair, holding her head. The unchecked longing on his face had her rising on tiptoe to kiss him.

"I wanted you then, too," she admitted passionately. "I just didn't want to admit how much."

He kissed her reverently. "You won't have to convince me again." Heat radiated from his body as he swept her into his arms and carried her down the hall to his bedroom.

He shut the door behind them. "I've wanted to be close to you, too, Brooke."

"Then make love to me, Nate," she said, her pulse pounding, as he slowly set her down. "Make love to me without a view toward tomorrow, or a glance back at yesterday." She wound her arms about his neck and kissed him persuasively. "Keep us in the here and now. Without rules or restrictions…"

Still kissing her, Nate drew her down onto the bed he'd been in too much of a rush that morning to make. When at last they broke apart, Brooke kicked off her sandals and lay back against the pillows. Nate shrugged out of his jacket, his tie. Unable to wait, he also kicked off his shoes and lay down beside her, looking unexpectedly vulnerable. "You're sure?"

Very. "I never do anything just for me," she whispered, lowering the wall around her heart a little more. She gave him a reason she thought he could accept. "I want you, just for me."

COMMON SENSE TOLD NATE to kiss Brooke until kissing was an end in itself. And then wait the traditional amount of time, until they knew each other thoroughly and they'd had a proper series of dates, before taking things to the next level again. He was old enough to know that was the safe way to proceed if he wanted to protect the investment he was making in their future together, especially if he wanted to convince her that what they had was much more than a fleeting sexual attraction. But when her hands skimmed over his entire body, there was no way to deny her. No way to stop the velvet caress of her lips pressing against his, any more than he could stop the burgeoning pressure against his fly. He wanted her, too.

And it wasn't just lust, as she wanted to think….

He needed her, needed this. Needed to discover the softness of her skin beneath her clothes, the warmth of her body, the jump in her pulse every time they connected. She was absolutely exquisite. Urging him on, trapping him with the sleek muscles of her long, slender thighs, she caressed him evocatively with her hands. She twisted beneath him, cupping his buttocks, molding her body to his, until they were both on fire.

The first time, he had seduced her. Now she was seducing him.

And still his hands rubbed down her back, claiming, exploring. The gentle curve of her hips, the swell of her breasts, the delicate skin between her thighs...

He followed the caress of his hands with the homage of his tongue, the adoration of his mouth. She arched her back and sucked in her breath. And then that, too, was too much.

He moved upward, claiming her mouth again, claiming her.

She encircled his neck with her arms and refused to let go. She wrapped her legs around his waist, giving herself over to him completely. And all the while she made soft sounds of surrender in the back of her throat that drove him wild.

He lifted her hips. And then they were one.

Soft as silk, hot as fire. Tight. Wet. Wanton.

Together, they rode the wave.

Faster, harder. Soft and slow. Slower, hotter, wetter still. And then she was his, really his. Not just for now, he determined, clasping her close. But as long as she would have him.

BROOKE LAY WRAPPED IN Nate's arms. In his bed.

The first time they'd made love they'd ended up in hers. Now they were in his.

Both times, it had felt right.

The only difference was that this time she wasn't as scared.

Now she was actually contemplating letting Nate become a part of her life. *One step at a time*. Wasn't that what she always told Cole? You can do anything if you break it down, and take it slowly?

On the floor beside them a humming began.

Recognizing the sound of a vibrating cell phone, Brooke lifted her head. Her phone was still set to ring. "That has to be for you."

Nate's eyes remained closed. "Let 'em leave a message."

She peered at him playfully, between her spread fingers. "Are you sure you're a CEO?"

The phone buzzed again.

The next thought occurred to both of them simultaneously. "What if it's...?"

"One of the kids." Nate let her go long enough to roll over and capture the offending electronic device.

He rolled back onto the pillows, lifting the screen where he could see it.

He hit a button, frowned, hit another button.

As their normal everyday life crept back in, Brooke found she needed reassurance. "Tell me that's not the kids with another field trip emergency."

"Actually, it's worse." The corners of Nate's mouth pulled down even more. "It's individual text messages— from my parents."

BROOKE SAT UP, holding the sheet against her bare breasts. Nate looked so distressed she had to ask, "Is everything all right with them?"

"I sent them an e-mail a few days ago and told them I was adopting Landry."

Brooke blinked. There were so many things wrong with that scenario she didn't know where to start. "And they're just now getting back to you?" she asked, aghast.

"They probably wanted to talk to each other, get on the same page, before they contacted me. And that wouldn't have been easy. I think I told you they live and work in different countries overseas."

What Nate hadn't discussed was the state of their union. Now, she had to wonder. "You didn't say…. Are they divorced?"

"No." Nate shrugged, as if that would be difficult to imagine, too. "They just live and work in different places," he explained. "It's been that way for the last, I don't know, ten or fifteen years."

"That must be hard."

"Honestly? I think they prefer it that way. Even when they worked in the same city they rarely saw each other. They're both married to their jobs."

"What was it like for you, when you were a kid?"

"I had nannies when I was younger. When I was in sixth grade, I switched to a residential private school, and I stayed at the school whenever they were out of town."

"Sounds…flexible." And as lonely, in certain ways, as her life as a foster child.

Funny, she'd thought she and Nate were so different. Now she saw that wasn't necessarily so. She swallowed the knot of building emotion in her throat.

Nate continued with a matter-of-fact shrug. "I understood they both had demanding jobs. And I never had any doubt that, despite the fact they weren't hands-on types in the parenting department, they loved me and wanted only the best for all of us."

Brooke took a deep breath and tried not to judge. It wasn't easy, given that this story was bringing out every protective, loving instinct in her and then some.

She traced the powerful outline of his shoulder with her fingertip and gently encouraged him to go on unburdening himself, the same way she had with him. "The best being?"

That rueful, cynically accepting smile came again. "Successful careers and professional lives for all of us, of course."

The Hutchinsons had certainly achieved that, from the sound of it, Brooke thought. Which brought them back to the text messages Nate's mom and dad had sent him. "So what did your parents say about your plan to adopt Landry?"

Nate peered at the screen. "My mother's text message says 'Nathaniel, if you want a child—and I'm not sure it's a good idea to go it alone given the tremendous business responsibilities you shoulder—then please get married and have one the old-fashioned way.'"

Brooke did her best not to wince. "And your dad?"

Nate read out loud, "'Is Landry your child? Because of course if he is, you have a duty to the boy. But if not, you have no business taking this on.'"

Nate showed the screen to her.

There were no loving overtures to soften the blow, just sanctimonious advice. Brooke's heart went out to Nate. "That's harsh."

He shrugged. "And direct. They're both CEO's…. So they tend to cut to the chase. I knew they wouldn't sugar-coat it, that they most likely would not approve of anything out of the ordinary on the personal front for me."

And yet he'd told them, anyway. Which meant part of him, the long-ago kid in him, still wanted their approval, even if he knew by now he would never get it. Not the way he wanted.

Brooke studied him. "What would have happened if you had e-mailed them that you were in love and getting married?" *If, for instance, you were ever to say that about us....*

"They would have offered formal congratulations and told me to get an ironclad prenup. After, of course, they did a thorough background check on not just my fiancée, but those around her."

Outrageous! Brooke rolled onto her stomach and rested her chin on her palm. "What did they think of Seraphina?" she asked curiously.

Nate frowned. "They saw her as a little too soft and sentimental to be a good executive wife, which was—in their estimation—what I needed for a successful climb up the career ladder."

Yet he had done it all by himself, Brooke noted proudly.

"So when the engagement ended?"

Nate tossed the phone aside and lay down again, facing her. His bare knee nudged hers beneath the covers. "They made no effort to disguise their relief," he continued, frankly. "They both felt I had avoided catastrophe."

Brooke studied his eyes for any clue to his feelings. "So to have Seraphina come back into your life, through her son…"

"Was not good news, not to them," Nate replied succinctly, then fell silent, brooding again.

There were mere inches between them. It felt like an ocean. Wanting to recapture some of their earlier closeness, Brooke reached out and covered his hand with hers. "What are you thinking?"

He gave her a rueful look, then ran a palm over his

face. "That I probably should have listened to my gut and not contacted my parents at all at this juncture. I should have waited until it was a fait accompli—when social pressure would have forced them to congratulate me, and welcome Landry to the family publicly. Knowing them, they'd find a way to make it all seem somehow noble and preordained."

Brooke's heart ached for him. She had an idea how much the lack of support from his parents must hurt. "It is noble and preordained, Nate. I've watched you with Landry. I know how right what you're doing is."

Although his expression lightened, a hint of sadness lingered in Nate's gaze. "Fortunately, my parents and I see each other so seldom now—once every year or two at most—that by the time we do get together again, Landry will officially be my son." He finished with his customary optimism.

Relieved that Nate had rebounded so quickly, Brooke lifted his hand and pressed a kiss to the back of his knuckles. "So they'll accept him and Landry will never have to know your parents disapproved."

The tension left Nate's body. He relaxed even more as she kissed his hand again. "That would be the plan."

Their eyes met. "You deserve better," she said quietly.

He took her arm and tugged her close. "I think I've finally got it." He bent his head and kissed her passionately "In you."

Chapter Eleven

"Why the frown?" Nate asked Brooke several hours later as he snuggled her closer, a wave of tenderness unlike anything he had ever felt radiating through him. She was so beautiful in her post-lovemaking dishabille. So beautiful all the time… It didn't matter whether she was in mom mode, on the job…or in his bed.

"I hate the thought of going back to work," she murmured, reluctantly glancing at her watch. "But with Holly Carson due here at one o'clock, to begin work on the dining-room mural, I've got to get going."

Nate had meetings, too. He rose and began to dress. "About this evening. I'll pick up the kids at camp and take them to the retirement village to see Jessalyn."

"I promised Landry I'd stop by to say hello to his great-grandmother, too. He wants her to get to know me."

Nate understood why. Brooke was one special woman. She'd already made a huge difference in Landry's life, by coaxing him out of his shell. "Then why don't we go over together to pick them up after the visit. Around seven o'clock?"

Surprise registered in Brooke's eyes. "You're not going to stay for the visit?"

Nate would have, had he been invited. "Landry thought it might go better with just him and Cole there. But he wanted me to stop in and say hello at the end of their time together."

"Then let's go together," Brooke said.

"Maybe stop for dinner out afterward?" Nate suggested, aware how much the four of them were beginning to feel like family.

Brooke smiled in a way that warmed his heart. "Sounds like a plan."

The rest of the day flew by. Nate picked up the guys as scheduled, at five o'clock, when camp ended. As usual, Landry and Cole spent the entire time talking, while Nate drove. But now he was occasionally included in the conversation about digital imaging and computer conversions.

"You sure you don't want me to go in?" Nate asked, pulling up in front of the entrance to the retirement home.

Landry nodded. "We can handle it. But—" he paused, sounding as if his heart was in his throat "—thanks for offering, Nate." Gaze averted, the boy got out of the car.

Cole followed. With their heads close together, they strolled toward the entrance. Nate thought—but couldn't be sure—that he saw Landry wipe a tear from the corner of his eye.

No doubt about it. This was a big day...for all of them.

"EVERYTHING OKAY?" Brooke asked, when Nate swung by the mansion to pick her up. He looked distracted, and concerned in a way he hadn't been when they had parted earlier that afternoon.

For a second she thought he wouldn't answer. Finally, he said, "I hope Landry's visit with Jessalyn is going well."

Brooke grinned, hearing the worry in his voice. "You sound like such a dad," she teased, and it was so good to see and hear. "Worrying—often unnecessarily—is what we parents do best," she explained when he shot her a sidelong glance.

He grinned as they walked toward his Jaguar. "Is that what this is?"

Brooke let her shoulder brush him in a playful nudge. "Doesn't feel familiar, huh?"

He wrapped his arm about her shoulder and pulled her close to his side. "It's beginning to," he whispered in her ear.

When they reached his sedan, he continued around to the passenger side. Trying not to make too much of the fact that he was opening her door for her, the way he would have had they been on an actual date, Brooke slid into the car, settled into the leather seat and smoothed her skirt over her knees. "I'm sure Landry and Cole are both doing fine." She paused to look up at him. "Otherwise, we would have heard. Cole would have called me on his cell phone."

Nate came around to the driver's side and slipped behind the wheel. "I wasn't aware he had a phone of his own."

"He doesn't use it a lot. He's not at the age where he spends a lot of time talking on the phone. But I feel better knowing he has it, in case of an emergency, or if anything unexpected comes up."

"I should probably get Landry one." Nate frowned, as if he felt he had failed. "I hadn't thought of that."

"I'm sure he'd appreciate it." Brooke opened up her purse and removed her notebook.

"I'll talk to him about it this evening," Nate vowed.

"In the meantime, I'd like to update you on where we stand with the makeover." She consulted her notes.

"So all you have left to do is add accessories and artwork and finish the formal dining room," Nate concluded, when her recitation was complete.

Brooke nodded. "With the exception of the mural,

which is going to take a few weeks, I'll be done by Friday evening. Which is good, because I start another job next Wednesday, and I need a couple of days off to handle things I've let slide at home."

Nate parked in front of the assisted-living center. "You're welcome to stay in the caretaker's cottage as long as you like," he offered as he cut the motor.

"Thank you, but it's time Cole and I head home. Especially since…"

He guessed correctly where the conversation was headed. "We've become lovers."

Brooke thrilled to hear him say that out loud. Still, Nate was a man with a reputation for having dated a lot of women. She released the latch on her shoulder harness and turned toward him. Suddenly, her heart was pounding. Her palms were damp. "*Is* that what we are?"

With his marine-blue eyes glittering warmly, he put his hand on hers and murmured, "I guess now is as good a time as any to make my pitch." He paused, looking sexy and unutterably masculine. She felt another lightning bolt surge of attraction. "I want us to come out of the shadows. Make it official. And start being seen together publicly."

"Are we talking about dating?"

His confident smile widened. "Call it whatever you want. As long as we're exclusive."

It was a tempting invitation. If their lives hadn't been so complicated, she would have jumped on it. As it was, it felt as if they were moving too fast. And it scared her. "That's a little more than just dating."

He nodded, accepting her assessment. His eyes swept the length of her, then returned with laser accuracy to her face. "And I hope you want that, too."

Despite what she had tried to tell herself earlier, Brooke had to admit she wouldn't have made love with Nate if her feelings for him hadn't been serious. The question was, would he have gone after her if he hadn't needed her to help him connect with his "son"? The last thing she wanted either of them to do was mistake need for love. And there was no doubt Nate—and Landry—had needed her the last couple of weeks. Just as she and Cole had benefited immensely from having Nate and Landry in their lives.

"Aren't we skipping a few steps?" she asked gently, as her customary common sense reasserted itself. She didn't want to make the same mistake she had made with Seamus. He'd been a serial dater, too, with a reputation for never being satisfied with any one woman until Brooke came along. And look how that had worked out….

She knew she wouldn't be able to bear it if Nate ever looked at her the way her late husband had—with sadness and disappointment, and then later, with avoidance and detachment.

She couldn't bear another mistake in the marriage department. She doubted Nate wanted another failed romantic relationship, either.

"I know what I want," he said quietly, with the drive and focus she was beginning to know so well. "And that's you." He paused, his emotional armor going up once again. "The question is—what do you want?"

"Time," Brooke answered honestly. *To make sure our feelings are real and lasting.* She swallowed painfully. "And enough space to figure this all out."

IT WASN'T THE ANSWER Nate was looking for, but it left the window for more wide open, and that was better than all-out rejection. He forced himself to sacrifice his own timetable and desires in favor of hers. "Take all the time you need," he told her gently.

Brooke regarded him with wonder in her golden-brown eyes. "You mean that."

Although he had once sworn he would never open his heart to another woman who didn't feel everything he did, Nate was suddenly willing to wait as long as it took. Which was another sign of how important Brooke was to him. "I do," he told her sincerely.

Her smile lit up his day. Visibly relieved, she squeezed his hand. Together, they got out of the car and went inside to find their sons.

Cole and Landry were in the visitors room, a large light and airy space filled with comfortable tables and chairs. Jessalyn was holding court with the two young men, chatting away and laughing.

She looked radiant, and much more energetic than the last time Nate and Brooke had seen her. He couldn't help but note that Landry appeared much healthier and happier, too.

"Thank you for bringing the boys to see me," Jessalyn said as Nate approached.

"It was my pleasure."

"We told Gran that we'd visit again on Saturday morning," Landry said. "It's okay, isn't it?"

Nate nodded. He had been hoping Landry and Jessalyn would make up. "It's more than okay."

Nate and Brooke stayed to visit for a while, and then all four of them headed out to the car. Since it was nearly 8:00 p.m., the boys were ravenous. After a brief consultation, they headed for P. F. Chang's.

"I'm glad you visited your great-grandmother," Nate said, after they had all studied the menu and placed their orders.

"I thought seeing her in an old people's home would be awful," Landry admitted with a rueful twist of his lips.

"That she'd be just sitting around waiting to die. But it was actually pretty nice. I can see that she's better off with all the nurses, and people her own age and stuff. Anyway—" he ducked his head "—I guess I don't have to feel like I deserted her anymore."

Nate had assumed—wrongly, he now knew—that it was the other way around, that it was Landry who had felt abandoned. "I imagine it comforted your great-grandmother to see you looking so good, too," he soothed.

Landry nodded. "She thinks it's clear I'm where I'm supposed to be now."

The question was, what did Landry think? Nate wondered.

The teen's brow furrowed. "Did you hear anything about the DNA test yet?"

"We probably won't learn anything until early next week." Nate wasn't about to protest any turn of events that would buy him more time to convince Landry that he belonged with him.

The teen fiddled with the chopsticks next to his plate. "What about your lawyer and that court thing we've got to do?"

"Ms. Tanous will file the papers as soon as we tell her we're ready."

Landry nodded, taking it all in.

Cole looked uneasy, as if he felt for his friend.

Brooke appeared about to intervene, but then Landry leaned forward and asked, "Do you think I'm more like you, Nate? Or Lawrence? 'Cause I've been thinking I'm a lot like you, in that I like to make decisions and be in charge of stuff."

Surprised and pleased by the comparison, Nate smiled. "You want to run your own company one day?"

"Maybe," he acknowledged shyly.

Cole chuckled. "I can totally see you calling all the shots. You're bossy, man."

Landry grinned and elbowed him.

"Always telling me what to do," Cole added.

The two boys pretended to fight over the last dumpling. "That's cause I'm older."

"By one year!" Cole protested.

Landry let him have the dumpling, and ate a spring roll with spicy orange sauce instead. "One year's a lot, especially between middle and high school."

His mouth still full, Cole conceded the point by mugging comically.

"So anyway—" Landry leaned toward Nate and continued his quest for information "—am I more like my dad or you in terms of personality? 'Cause I'm not really a funny guy. I like to laugh, but I'm never the one coming up with the jokes."

"Me, either," Nate said. He usually left that to people with true comic ability.

"I mean, I know I look like my mom," Landry continued earnestly. "I've got her hair and eye color and all that."

"Yes, you do," Nate said. Landry had all of Seraphina's good qualities.

"So that doesn't really tell us anything. It'd be easier, I guess, if I had any real memories of Lawrence, but all I've got are a couple of pictures my mom gave me, from when they were still together." Landry reached into his back pocket, withdrew his wallet. He brought out two tattered color photos of Lawrence and Seraphina. They had their arms around each other in both photos, and appeared to be laughing and having a good time. "It just feels weird, not to know more about him," the boy admitted.

Nate wanted to say it wasn't important, but clearly it was to Landry. The teenager was searching for connection. It was only fair, Nate thought, that he do what he could to ease the pain. "I'll see what I can dig up for you," he promised.

A SEARCH ON YouTube that night turned up nothing on Lawrence. Ditto the Google, Yahoo and Safari Internet search engines. Frustrated, Nate went on to bed. The next day, over a working lunch, he talked to the guys about it.

"You could have Laura Tillman's private detective agency see what they could find, if you really want to go that route," Travis advised.

Nate trusted the guys, who were all great dads in their own right. "You think it's a mistake to be looking backward?" he asked.

Dan, the veteran parent of teenagers, shrugged, and predicted, "If the DNA results come back that way, you won't have a choice."

Nate knew Dan had shepherded his own kids through their fair share of biological-parent-induced hurt. It had been excruciating—and unfair.

"In the meantime, maybe you should concentrate on answering Landry's questions, while keeping him focused on his future with you," Jack said, with his customary protectiveness toward family.

"You're what he needs. And the sooner he realizes that, the better," Grady agreed.

Nate relaxed. "I think he already is." He related everything else that had happened in the previous few days.

"We should celebrate," Grady said.

"And I know just the way," Nate replied. Now all he had to do was talk Brooke into it.

"YOU WANT TO HAVE A PARTY here on Saturday?" Brooke asked, when she and Nate went in to look at the mural sketched on the dining-room wall.

Holly wanted Nate's approval before she actually started painting.

Nate studied the historical pictorial of Fort Worth, from the early days to the present, ending with the current skyline and the skyscraper that housed One Trinity River Place, home to Nate's business.

He gave the drawing his seal of approval, then turned back to Brooke. "It'll be sort of a home makeover slash Father's Day celebration with all the guys and their families. And of course, I want you and Cole to be here, too."

The enthusiasm he expected to see on Brooke's face was nowhere to be found. "It might be kind of awkward, given the fact that Cole's dad won't be here."

Nate bit back an oath. How could he have made such a blunder? Then again, considering his own family-challenged upbringing, how could he not? Nate exhaled slowly, wondering how to get out of this. "I'm sorry…. I didn't think about that." The last thing he wanted to do was resurrect Cole's grief.

Brooke paused, as if having second thoughts. "The truth is—we never did much to celebrate that particular holiday. It wasn't one Seamus put much stock in. Let me ask Cole, see how he feels." She slipped off to do so before Nate could protest.

He went back to studying the mural, then walked through the entire first floor of the mansion. Soft, earth-toned hues were on all the walls. Warm rugs livened up the wide plank floors. Comfortable furniture and fun, family-oriented accessories abounded. There were flowers in the front hall. A bowl of fresh fruit on the kitchen counter. And little touches that said Brooke everywhere he looked.

She returned, a jubilant expression on her face. "Cole wants to attend the party, and so does Landry."

"Even knowing we plan to celebrate Father's Day?" Nate asked.

She shrugged, evidently as surprised as he was. "Especially knowing that, they both said. They think it's awesome you're going to be a dad, too."

Contentment flowed through Nate. "So Landry is finally getting used to the idea of me adopting him?"

Brooke nodded in approval. "Seeing Jessalyn happy in her new place seems to have given him permission to move on, too."

"Then I guess there's just one more question to be asked. Will you stay through the weekend and cohost the party with me?"

Chapter Twelve

"If it was just me," Brooke said, "I'd have no problem saying yes. But I have Cole and you have Landry to consider."

Once again, she had the strong intuition that Nate wanted to kiss her. Senses reeling, she stepped back.

He shoved his hands into his back pockets and rocked toward her. His expression was as steady and resolute as his voice. "I think they'd be okay with it."

"More than okay if things work out," Brooke conceded. She shifted her attention away from his washboard abs, what she knew was hidden behind his fly. "The problem is—" she forced her attention upward, to the handsome contours of Nate's face "—what if they don't?"

"Borrowing trouble?"

She shot him a get-with-the-program-before-we're-both-in-big-trouble look. "Being realistic. I'm getting ready to move back to my place. And you're coming up with ways to keep me—and Cole—here at least one more day." And while it was flattering, unexpected, and oh so romantic, it was also completely impractical.

Unless, of course, they wanted everyone, even the boys, to know they had a thing for each other, and she didn't... not just yet.

"Can you blame me?" Nate held her gaze with his

mesmerizing blue eyes, making her feel all hot and bothered inside. Slowly, a smile bloomed on his lips. "Life has been so much better since you arrived."

For me, too. "It's still not a prudent move to make." And she had let the fantasy of what could be guide her once before, into a hasty marriage that had fallen far short of expectation. For all their sakes, she didn't want to make the same mistake again.

"You and I are going to work out for the long haul, Brooke."

She so wanted to believe it. As if he knew that, Nate bent his head and kissed her sweetly. Longing swept through her, along with the intense feelings she had for him. She moaned, knowing that if they kept this up she wouldn't sleep all night, but lie awake wanting him. And she couldn't have that, either. Not when she had so many responsibilities to fulfill. She pressed her palms to his chest, wishing, at least for now, it was just the two of them. "Nate…"

He kissed her again, slowly, lingeringly. Then he swept his fingers through her hair and gazed deep into her eyes. "Just tell me you'll think about it," he urged softly, scoring his thumb across her lower lip with a tenderness that almost undid her completely.

"All right. But that's all I'm doing right now," she told him sternly. "Mulling it over."

He smiled and kissed her again, feeling victorious. "Good enough."

Aware that it was getting late, Brooke said good-night to Nate and went down to the caretaker's cottage.

Cole and Landry were where she had left them a few minutes before. Both were huddled on the couch in front of Cole's laptop computer, looking at the photos of their visit to the amusement park the previous weekend.

"I thought you guys were going to hit the shower," Brooke murmured.

"In a minute, Mom." Cole waved her over to join them. "Isn't this a great picture of Nate?"

Brooke perched on the back of the sofa behind them and studied the photo on-screen. Nate was standing in front of the last roller coaster they had ridden that day, his arms around Landry and Cole. All three of them were a little sunburned and windblown. The happiness they had been feeling was palpable. "I remember taking that one," she murmured.

"Here's one of you and us." Landry scrolled to the next image.

Brooke had been clowning around with both kids, hands framing her face, as if in a silent movie scream of fake terror as she lingered in front of the entrance to a kiddie ride that wouldn't have scared a six-year-old. Landry and Cole were both laughing and grinning from ear to ear.

"That was a really good day," Landry said softly. "One of the best I've ever had."

"For me, too," Cole murmured.

"It was for all of us." Brooke placed a comforting hand on a shoulder of each boy.

She would hold the memory close for a long time, and sensed they would, too.

The guys turned to her with beseeching grins. "Which brings us to our next request," Landry drawled. "Could you do us one more tiny little favor?"

FRIDAY MORNING, Brooke and the boys overslept. By the time Nate realized everyone in the caretaker's cottage was still asleep, and hastily woke them, it was a mad rush to get ready for camp and hurry out the door.

His calls to Brooke during the day went straight to voice

mail. Ditto hers to him. He had a stop to make on the way home from work, and it was seven o'clock before he pulled in the driveway.

To his surprise, Brooke was just arriving, too.

He got out of the car and headed for hers. In the rear seat, both boys waved and then ducked down. As he neared, he saw they were both zipping up the backpacks they'd taken to camp. The expressions on their faces were choirboy innocent as they piled out of the car.

"Hi, Nate." Cole didn't quite meet his eyes.

Landry's gaze focused on the ultracasual fist bump he gave Nate. "Hey, dude. What's happening?"

Exactly what I'd like to know, Nate thought, as Brooke got out from behind the steering wheel, her cheeks a lot more pink than usual, too. "Sorry I missed all your calls today," she said. Then, realizing they had company, and catching herself, she added, "I assume you wanted to talk about the plans for the party here tomorrow."

"I do." But that wasn't why Nate had called her. He had dialed her number because he wanted to hear her voice. The intense need for connection was new to him. And yet satisfying, too.

"I guess you-all stopped and had dinner on the way home from camp," Nate said, disappointed they wouldn't all be eating together, as had become the custom.

"Uh…actually, no, we didn't." Brooke abruptly rummaged through her purse and came up with nothing, before zipping it closed again. "I just… I had a few errands to run and the boys graciously agreed to go with me," she murmured, still averting her gaze.

Was she lying to him? Nate wondered. Or at the very least, not telling him something?

He hadn't had a woman *not* look at him quite that

way since Seraphina had been ducking out on him with Lawrence, behind the scenes....

"But I imagine the boys are hungry." Brooke rambled on, as even more color flooded her high, sculpted cheeks.

"Very hungry," they chimed in.

"You want to go out?" Nate asked, more than happy to treat them all.

Shrugs all around. Again, to Nate's frustration, something wordless—and private—passed between Brooke and the boys. "Actually, we've got some stuff to do," Cole murmured finally, taking the lead. "But—" he looked at his mom, silently pleading "—if you and Nate want to go out and get something and bring it back, that would be good."

Brooke appeared to understand whatever Cole was telling her. "No problem," she said. "Nate, we'll go together. And let's make it a steak-house night." She named a place a good thirty minutes away.

Nate countered, "We could go to Morty's—it's a lot closer. If the guys are hungry."

The boys looked at Brooke. "Uh...we can wait," Cole said.

"Yeah, we'll have a granola bar or something in the meantime." Landry stuffed his hands into the pockets of his khaki shorts.

Brooke's usual admonishment not to eat too much right before dinner never came.

She smiled and, grasping Nate's elbow, guided him in the direction she wanted him to go.

"So what's going on?" Nate asked, as he and Brooke got in the car and headed for her favorite steak place, on the other side of town.

She flashed him a look of pure confusion.

Nate didn't buy her naivete for a moment. Drolly, he explained, "I'd say the kids were matchmaking, but they don't know we're together. So there has to be another reason they want us both out of the cottage for a good long while."

She took a deep breath, her soft breasts rising and falling beneath her tailored cotton blouse. She made a show of tugging her business-casual skirt down to her knees. "Look. Obviously the boys are behaving a bit melodramatic tonight."

"Because?"

"Because they're kids and they're excited about this project they're working on."

"For camp?" Nate persisted.

Brooke lifted a silencing palm. She wrinkled her nose into a comical expression. Chuckling, she said, "I can't tell you anything else so you need to stop asking questions."

While they waited at the traffic light, Nate slanted a glance at her trim ankles and fantastically shaped calves. "Obviously you know what Cole and Landry are up to."

"Yes." Brooke watched the red turn to green. She gestured, indicating it was safe for him to go. "I do."

Nate doubled-checked the road, then went through the intersection. As soon as it was safe, he pulled over and put the car in Park.

In the soft light of a summer evening, her classically beautiful features were more pronounced. In deference to the heat of the June day, she'd swept her glossy hair into a clip at the back of her head. Tendrils escaped to frame her face and neck.

Nate draped his arm along the seat, behind her head. "Then why can't I know?" He hated being excluded. It reminded him of his youth.

Brooke released her seat belt and scooted toward him.

She kissed him until all he could think and feel and want was her.

"I promise you," she murmured eventually, pressing closer, "if you do as I ask and let the boys do what they need to do tonight, they'll be happy campers and so will we."

That sounded even more mysterious. But in a good way.

He relaxed as Brooke slipped back into her seat and refastened her safety belt. He couldn't resist the merry look in her golden-brown eyes. He turned to her with a wink. "Okay, then. Your wish is my command."

"THAT WAS A GREAT dinner!" Cole exclaimed an hour and a half later, when four steaks, nearly a dozen yeast rolls with butter, and a round of salads and desserts had been consumed. He grinned with thirteen-year-old exuberance. "Thanks, Nate."

Landry patted his full belly, looking equally content. "Yeah, thanks."

It still amazed Nate how much these guys could eat. They were true bottomless pits. They took so much pleasure in eating that it was a privilege supplying them with food. Particularly when Nate contrasted this evening's meal with Landry's first dinner at the mansion, twelve days before.

Aware that he wasn't the only one harboring a secret that evening, Nate rose leisurely from his seat. "It's not the only thing I have for you guys tonight."

Although the boys hadn't revealed what they had been working on earlier, their brows lifted in interest.

Nate walked over to his briefcase and withdrew two BlackBerry Smartphones. He carried them over to the boys and wordlessly handed one to each, along with the instruction manuals. The teens stared at him, not understanding. "They're all programmed and ready to go," Nate said.

Cole's jaw dropped. The cell phone he carried now was a basic model, with very limited capability. Landry didn't have a phone at all.

"Of course, you can use them to make calls," Nate told them proudly. "But you can also check your e-mail, text message, browse the Web, use the GPS, take and store photos, even transfer programs and watch them. I've already put in your mother's cell phone and home numbers, and all of mine. The manuals will tell you how to add those of your friends."

The boys continued staring at their phones in sheer amazement.

"Wow," Cole said finally.

"I can't believe I've got something like this," Landry murmured, his eyes glimmering with moisture.

Afraid if he looked directly at Landry, he'd tear up, too, Nate turned and caught a glimpse of Brooke's inexplicably shocked expression, and went back to his briefcase. "And I have one other thing," he told the boys, knowing this would mean even more, at least to Landry. "I was able to get some old footage from one of the comedy clubs in town. Apparently, they tape all their open-mike nights and hold on to the video, just in case someone later becomes really famous. They had a couple of the routines Miles Lawrence did. I thought you might like to watch them."

AT THE BOYS' INSISTENCE, all four of them trooped up to the media room. The videos were slipped into the DVD player. They all sat down to watch.

Miles Lawrence was tall—like Nate and Landry. Handsome in a slightly disheveled, ne'er-do-well frat boy way—and hysterically funny. They were all chuckling as they watched, even Nate.

As he watched the routine about unrequited love, it was clear Landry felt comforted. When the last bit ended, he sat there a moment, silent, then murmured, "I guess I see why my mom fell so hard for him."

Then, realizing the impact of his words, he froze in horror and turned to Nate. "Oh, man, I—"

"I know what you mean," Nate said kindly. "Miles was a funny guy. And I think your mom loved him very much."

"It just wasn't a love that was returned," Landry reflected with a swiftness that indicated he had spent a fair amount of time thinking about this. "'Cause otherwise Miles would have married her, don't you think?"

For a moment, Brooke noted, Nate looked as if he was going to play that down. Then his expression changed to the one of forthright honesty she knew so well, and he said, "I think you're right—Miles didn't love your mother enough for a marriage to succeed—so they're probably lucky they didn't go down that road. But I also think, had he had an opportunity to get to know you—and realize what a gift it is to have a son—he would have done right by you, even if he and your mom never married. I think he would have been a *great* dad to you, Landry."

Brooke knew Nate sure wanted to be…and in so many ways, already was.

Once again Landry's eyes teared up. He nodded, seeming so choked up he was unable to get any words out. Then he turned back to the TV and mumbled to Cole, "Let's watch it one more time, okay?"

"As many times as you want," Cole said.

Figuring now was as good a time as any to say what she needed to Nate—alone—Brooke sent him a look and inclined her head toward the hall. They walked out together.

Nate peered at her closely. "You okay?" he murmured.

Yes, Brooke thought. *And no.* "Let's walk out by the pool," she said instead.

He followed her down the stairs, out the back door, across the yard. "What is it?" he asked, when they finally reached the lagoon-style swimming area.

I think I'm falling in love with you....

But knowing now wasn't the time to make that admission, Brooke forced herself to return to the issue at hand. "I was going to read you the riot act about the Smartphone."

Nate looked stunned by the slight censure in her tone, then apologetic. He ran a palm across his jaw. "I gather I should have asked first."

Heck yes, he should have! "Nate, I know you meant well, but I can't give Cole gifts like that."

Nate shrugged, still not seeing the problem. He angled a thumb at his chest. "But I can."

Brooke's eyes were drawn to the smooth skin and curly tufts of black hair springing out of the open V of his shirt. Light-headed from the memories and images bombarding her, she drew a breath and stepped back. "I'm not even sure he should have anything that elaborate."

Nate studied her, some of the light exiting his blue eyes. "From me or in general?" he wondered aloud.

Brooke knew she was hurting his feelings, but it couldn't be helped. "Both," she answered bluntly.

"I'm sorry. I wanted Landry to have a phone."

Naturally, a well-to-do Nate wanted Landry to have the very best.

"And I didn't want to give him a gift and hand Cole nothing."

Brooke appreciated Nate's thoughtfulness, even if he still didn't see the emotional implications of his actions. "Landry is your son."

"That's the thing, Brooke. Cole feels like my son, too."

What could she say to that? She loved the way Nate treated Cole. Brooke's heart skipped a beat. "I'm fond of Landry, too."

Hope shone on Nate's face. "Then it's okay?"

She rolled her eyes in exasperation. "No! It's not! In the future, if you're going to do something like this, or you're even tempted to do so, you need to run it by me first."

"Fair enough."

Silence descended.

"Something else is on your mind."

"What you did just now for Landry—getting that recording for him, saying what you did about Miles—was really decent."

"Even if it wasn't one hundred percent true." Nate looked conflicted. "I misled him there at the end, when I said Lawrence would have appreciated him."

Brooke edged closer and slipped her hand in his. "Then why did you do it?"

Nate squeezed her fingers as he admitted in a low, troubled voice, "Because I couldn't stand to see him hurt." He paused, as if struggling with his conscience. "It's what I hope would have happened…."

"But you don't know for sure," Brooke interjected.

He turned to her, a beseeching look in his eyes. "I never understood why you would lie to protect your son. Until now." His lips compressed. "Because that's what I just did."

Afraid the boys might come out and see the clandestine show of affection, Brooke stepped back. "There are worse things."

Nate tore his eyes from the underwater lights and shimmering blue of the swimming pool amid the darkening night. "Are there?"

Unable to seek solace from his arms, Brooke let the warmth of the summer evening surround her. "Our boys may look like almost-adults," she told him softly, "but at heart they're still just kids in a lot of ways."

Kids who needed parents, Brooke thought. And Nate was turning out to be one fine one indeed.

"Mom?" Cole asked Saturday morning over breakfast, while Nate gave them a tutorial on their new phones. "Is it okay with you if Landry goes to the book publication party for Dad?"

Brooke looked up from the to-do list she was writing for their own casual party later that day. "Well, I—" she began.

"The other professors at the university won't mind, will they?" Cole persisted. "I want Landry to see who my dad was, too."

To her relief, Nate's expression remained blessedly inscrutable.

Which left the ball firmly in her court. How should she answer this? "Of course Landry can come—if they have the party," Brooke said finally.

Cole's brow furrowed. "Why *wouldn't* they have it?"

Time to fib, Brooke thought, her own conscience prickling. "There was some sort of scheduling problem they were trying to work out, last I heard." *Based on whether they could figure out if there was any validity to the plagiarism claim.*

"So you don't know if they are going to have it or not?" Cole pressed.

Brooke was finally able to answer honestly. She looked him in the eye. "I'm still waiting to hear."

"Well, whenever they do have it, I want to go," Cole stated firmly. "And I want Landry to come with us, too."

"So noted." Brooke wasn't about to engage in an argument about the hypothetical. Ignoring Nate's under-the-radar look—which seemed to indicate she had done something wrong—she continued, "In the meantime, I've got a ton of grocery shopping to do." She smiled brightly. "Who wants to come with me?"

Cole and Landry exchanged looks. "Uh, we've got that project to work on," Cole said. "We didn't finish it yet."

Nate lifted a brow, perplexed. "What project?"

The boys again traded glances, and shrugged. "Just something we're working on," Landry said vaguely.

"So can we opt out?" Cole asked.

Knowing exactly what they were up to, she smiled and nodded, then turned to Nate. "Can you come with me, then?"

He stood agreeably. Still curious, but cool enough not to ask. "You bet."

Brooke grabbed her list and her purse. She turned to the boys, who were already half out the door, their Smartphones in hand. "Just be warned that when I get back I will be enlisting your help."

They nodded in agreement and waved her off.

"Alone at last," Nate teased as they hit the driveway.

He made it sound so sexy! If only it could have been that way. But with a party set to start in a matter of hours, that wasn't an option. She peered at him playfully. "I didn't plan this."

He wrinkled his nose. "I wish you had."

So, thought Brooke wistfully as they set off to complete their chores, did she.

"I DON'T KNOW WHAT'S better," Grady McCabe said hours later, as he and the other guys finished the tour of Nate's redecorated home. "The changes Brooke brought to the living quarters or the change she brought to you."

Nate stopped at the cooler they'd put on the patio, and handed out beers. "My happiness shows, hmm?"

"Landry looks pretty content, too." Dan nodded at the badminton net set up on the sport court. Cole and Landry were dividing the other kids into teams.

"He's a great kid," Nate said proudly.

"That he is," Dan said. The others all nodded in agreement.

"So what's the deal with Brooke?" Jack asked, deadpan. "You-all out of the closet yet?"

Chuckles abounded.

"No." Nate elbowed the guys closest to him and kept his voice purposefully low. "She thinks all the kids need to know right now is that the two of us have developed a very casual platonic friendship."

Travis grunted. "Which might be fine if the kids weren't very bright, but…"

"You're right—they're sharp as a tack," Nate agreed. "And I'm afraid they're going to pick up on something." A look, a touch, the most inane comment… He shook his head in frustration. "But she still won't budge."

"Why not?" Dan helped himself to guacamole and chips. "From what I've noticed—and from what she's told Emily—it looks like she really has a thing for you."

Nate had only to think about the passionate way Brooke made love with him to realize the validity of that. "She does. And I have a thing for her that goes beyond anything I've ever felt."

The guys, having all been there themselves with their wives, grinned. "So what's the problem?" Grady teased.

That much, at least, was easy, Nate thought. "Deep down, Brooke doesn't trust romantic love. She sees it as a fleeting, ephemeral thing."

Travis shrugged. "It probably was, in her marriage. It won't be the same for the two of you. Especially if you're this serious."

He was. Frustrated, Nate took a swig of his beer and glanced over at Brooke as she and the other women emerged from their tour of the house. With sunlight glinting off her hair, and her eyes bright with laughter, she was more beautiful than ever. "I want to tell the world." Nate worked to contain his disappointment when the women stopped to talk once again. "But she's not ready yet."

"It'll happen," Grady predicted with the legendary McCabe knowledge of male-female dynamics. He studied Brooke, and the way she looked so completely at home on Nate's turf, then turned back to his pal. "Maybe sooner than you think…"

Nate sure as heck hoped so. He was a patient man, but only to a point.

Chapter Thirteen

On Sunday morning, Brooke met Nate as he headed for the caretaker's cottage. Swiftly, she moved to block his path, then adopted the stance of a baseball outfielder protecting a base. "You can't go in there."

Nate chuckled at her playful gesture and flashed a perplexed smile. He stopped and folded his arms across his chest. "You want to tell me why?" He cocked his head. "Or am I supposed to guess?"

Brooke looped her arm through his, guided him into a one-hundred-eighty-degree turn and steered him toward the swimming pool, where she sank down on the foot of a chaise. He took the one next to her.

"Since it's our last morning here, Landry and Cole thought they should do something special." She slipped off her flip-flops and flexed her bare toes on the sun-warmed concrete. Her hot-pink nail polish glinted in the sunshine. "So they're cooking breakfast for all of us."

"Wow." Like her, Nate couldn't help but be impressed.

It was unusual. Teenage boys generally spent most of their time in the kitchen either eating or asking to be fed. They were also loath to do chores of any kind. Yet there they were, working like a well-oiled team toward a common goal. Miracles, it seemed, would never cease, at least where the four of them were concerned.

"They said they'd call us when it's ready," Brooke continued.

His lips compressed into a thoughtful line, as if he sensed there was more to this than she was saying thus far. "Can't wait."

Fearing if she continued looking into his eyes, she would give away the real reason behind the "family fete," Brooke turned her glance away. She wondered what Nate's reaction was going to be when he saw the entire surprise Cole and Landry had dreamed up Thursday evening, and spent most of the weekend working on behind closed doors.

Nate stood and moved restlessly to the edge of the pool. For a while he looked down at the shimmering water, then turned and strolled back. "I can't believe you have been here for almost two weeks." He stopped just short of her, towering over her.

Brooke flushed. "Time flies when you're having fun."

Nate reached for her hand and pulled her to her feet. "And it has been fun," he murmured softly, still looking down at her.

She could tell he was thinking about kissing her.

She knew, because she was thinking about kissing him.

The door to the cottage banged open, prompting them to move surreptitiously apart.

"Mom! Nate!" Cole shouted, clearly oblivious to the impulsive show of affection that would have "outed" them to the boys, had temptation gotten the best of them yet again.

"Come on!" Landry added. "It's going to get cold!"

Nate shrugged. He still looked as if he wanted to kiss her. "You heard the chefs."

Feeling hot and bothered all over, Brooke pivoted and strolled with Nate toward the cottage.

Inside, the table had been set. Glasses of juice and steaming cups of coffee sat beside their plates. Buttered toast, slightly charred eggs and undercooked bacon completed the repast. In the center of the awkwardly laid table was a bouquet of flowers that had been picked from the beds along the front of the house. That touch, Brooke figured, had been more for her than Nate.

Nate nodded approvingly at the kids' efforts, and helped Brooke into her chair. "Looks great, guys."

The boys grinned from ear to ear, knowing—as did Brooke—that the biggest revelation was yet to come.

The three of them sat down in turn. "So anyway…we were thinking—" Cole began his pitch, catching her off guard, too "—there's really no reason Mom and I need to rush off today, it being the weekend and all…."

Landry continued, "So maybe the four of us could just hang out together this morning and go see a movie or something this afternoon."

Brooke lifted a brow. She had an idea where this campaign was going.

"That's a great idea!" Nate enthused. "Brooke?"

Emotion warred with common sense. Her feelings for Nate won. "That's fine, but we really have to get our stuff together and go home after that, Cole," she warned. It was going to be hard enough to leave as it was.

Nate understood the difficulty they were facing. He turned to the boys compassionately. "It's not as if we won't see each other after that," he said. "We'll see each other all the time. In fact, I'd like to continue carpooling to camp for the rest of the summer."

"It's a little out of the way," Brooke noted.

Nate eyed her expectantly. "The extra drive time will give us all time to talk."

"Sounds good to me!" Cole exclaimed.

"Me, too!" Landry said.

To Brooke, as well, if she was honest. She just wished she didn't harbor so many fears about getting in too deep.... She blew out an exasperated breath. "Make that me, three...."

The boys grinned victoriously, then turned back to Nate. "What movie do you want to see?" Landry asked, hero worship glowing on his young face.

"Depends on what's showing," Nate said.

Cole pulled out his new BlackBerry. "I'll look it up on the Internet."

Options were discussed throughout the rest of the meal. They finally decided to see an action-adventure film starring a group of teenagers.

The meal over, their plans set, Nate stood. "I'll do the dishes this morning."

The boys rushed to intervene. "You can't do that," they said in unison.

Nate grimaced in confusion. "Why not?"

More furtive looks were exchanged. "Wait here!" They told him, then disappeared into their respective bedrooms.

"Why don't you take a seat on the couch?" Brooke suggested, knowing what was next.

More baffled than ever, Nate let her lead him there.

The boys burst back out, hands behind their back. Expressions jubilant, they thrust two presents at him. "Happy Father's Day!"

For the briefest of seconds, Brooke thought Nate was going to lose it. She was close herself, with her throat closing up and sentimental tears welling in her eyes. Wary of doing anything that would detract from the pure sweetness of this moment for any of them, she sucked in a breath and worked valiantly to put her own emotions on hold.

Fortunately, the three males were so wrapped up in their gift giving and receiving they were oblivious to her reaction. Silence reigned as the two boys focused solely on the recipient of their admiration and affection. And in that moment, Nate looked like the proud and grateful father *both* kids needed him to be. Even Cole…

Nate shook his head, cleared his throat. "I'm…over-whelmed," he managed to say finally.

So were the boys, Brooke noted happily. Everything was working out so well.

Predictably, the older, streetwise Landry was the first to get it together. He discreetly rubbed a hand beneath his eye. "You can't be overwhelmed until you open it," he chided Nate.

Beside him, Cole was surreptitiously blotting his eyes, too. "Mine first," he said. When Landry looked less than pleased, Cole added, "We're saving the best for last!"

Landry's face split into a wide grin. "True."

Nate tore into the wrapping appreciatively. The top of the gift box bore the words Parent Survival Kit.

"I figured you might need it, you being new at this stuff and all," Cole teased.

Chuckling, Nate opened the box. Inside were all the essentials. *A Father's Guide to Understanding his Teenage Son*—written in guyspeak, by a famous comedian they all admired. Next up was a detailed playlist of all the essential tunes, and can't-miss movies and TV shows, meticulously compiled by both boys. And an invitation to join them in the enjoyment of said entertainment anytime. Earplugs, for when he couldn't stand the noise. A schedule for the Texas Rangers baseball games, with an IOU for tickets to the game of his choice. And last but not least, a how-to guide and promise of further hands-on tutorials designed to bring him up to speed on his interactive-video-game-playing skills so he would be better able to compete in family tournaments.

"Right now, we kind of feel like we're taking advantage of you," Cole teased.

Nate shook his head, visibly pleased. "This is great. Thank you."

Cole and Landry bumped fists. "It's officially from me, but we came up with all the stuff together."

They were so much like brothers, Brooke thought. Always giving exactly what the other needed...

"But this one is just from me," Landry said, handing over the second present.

Nate sent him a grateful look and opened it.

Inside was a photo of Landry and Nate, taken at the amusement park. They were standing with their arms around each other, exuding happiness. The personally engraved message on the sterling silver frame said, "Happy Father's Day, to the Best Dad Ever."

NATE HAD NEVER BEEN the kind of guy who cried happy tears. Damned if he wasn't tempted to change that, here and now. Deciding to put better use to the emotion, he stood, grabbed both boys and pulled them into a fierce group hug. Throat tight, he held them there, putting all the love he felt for them—and he did love both of the boys—into the single gesture. They hugged him back just as fiercely.

Brooke, overcome, started to walk away.

Not about to let her miss out on what was turning into a very satisfying exchange, Nate grabbed her, too, and pulled her into the middle. As she joined in the embrace, the sound that came out of her mouth was half laugh, half sob.

It brought the boys up short. "Mom!" Cole demanded, shocked. "Are you crying?"

"Of course not," she fibbed tearfully.

Cole shook his head, ignoring the fact he and Landry had been all choked up just seconds earlier. "You're not supposed to cry! This is a happy occasion!"

"I know." Brooke patted her cheeks with her splayed fingertips. "I can't help it!" she complained, her chin quivering. "You-all are just so sweet."

Cole and Landry groaned as if in terrible pain.

Brooke teared up even more....

Nate wasn't sure what this was about. More than the sentimentality of the occasion and the gifts, certainly... He touched both boys on the shoulder. "Why don't you give your mom a moment?" he suggested.

Appearing all too glad to be away from the show of unchecked emotion before they got sucked in, too, they acquiesced. "We'll be over at the main house, playing video games," Landry said.

"Good idea," Nate told him, while Brooke continued to cry.

Nate waited until the boys had crossed the lawn and disappeared into the house, then went back into the cottage and pulled Brooke into his arms. "Hey, now," he said, patting her back. "It's okay."

"More than okay." She buried her head in his shoulder. Her voice was muffled against his shirt. "That's the problem."

Nate led her to the kitchen and guided her into the walk-in pantry, so that even if the boys slammed back into the house unexpectantly, he and Brooke would have a chance to move apart before being seen. He steadied her with a gentle hand on her waist. "You're going to have to explain that one."

She stood close to him and tilted her face up to his. "Cole adores you so much."

He pressed a tender hand to her cheek, then smoothed it through her hair. "I love him, too."

She went very still. With a conflicted look in her eyes, she searched his face. "You do, don't you?"

Nate wondered if she was feeling as deprived of intimacy and affection as he was. "Yes. Cole's a great kid. He got into my heart in no time." *Same as you...* But sensing she wasn't ready to hear that just yet, he said only, "Same as Landry."

Brooke extricated herself from his possessive grasp and stepped aside. "I worry—"

He came closer and pressed a finger to her lips. "Stop."

Her shoulders stiff, she continued anyway "—what will happen if you and I—"

Nate wouldn't consider the possibility that what they shared might end. He wrapped his arms around her yet again. Holding her close, he promised, "I'm going to be there for him, whenever...however he needs me, Brooke." The raw vulnerability in her face gave him the courage to add, "I'm going to do the same thing for you. And for Landry."

She regarded him soberly. "You mean that, don't you?"

Hell yes. Nate nodded. "You've got my word." He bent to kiss her, and she wound her arms about his neck and melted against him in sweet surrender.

Knowing it was either stop now or continue kissing her and end up making love to her under far less than ideal circumstances, he paused and drew back. That would happen soon, at the appropriate time. But for now, it was important that she had confided in him. It meant a lot that he could confide at least part of what he was thinking and feeling in turn.

Certain they could build on that foundation, he smiled and took her hand. "Let's go find the boys."

SUNDAY EVENING, Cole roamed the house like a prisoner in a cell. It was still Father's Day, but the father figure most recently in his life was nowhere close. "You said we'd be happy coming back home," he told Brooke disconsolately.

Normally, we would be, Brooke thought morosely as she sorted through two weeks' worth of mail.

Of course, normally she wasn't involved in an openended love affair where the possibility of love hadn't even been broached…. And yet despite that, she had never felt happier than when she was with Nate.

Cole folded his arms across his chest. "Well, I'm not happy at all, Mom! I miss Nate and Landry!"

I miss them, too. More than I thought I would. But that didn't mean she should allow herself to rely on Nate and Landry to make her and Cole happy 24/7. That was her job, Brooke reminded herself sternly.

Still scowling, her son shoved his hands through his hair. "I wish we could have just stayed there."

Forced by circumstance to play the role of spoilsport, Brooke ignored her own yearning. "You know why we couldn't do that."

He snorted. "Because your job there is done, except for the dining-room mural, and we don't need to be on-site for that to happen. You just have to be available to troubleshoot if a problem comes up."

Brooke thought her repeated explanation had fallen on

deaf ears, she'd had to say it so many times. Pleased that it hadn't, she reminded him kindly, "You're going to see Landry and Nate tomorrow. I'm taking both of you boys to camp in the morning, and Nate is picking you up tomorrow evening." So it wasn't as if they had to cut off all contact, because that would have been way too tough for both kids. And herself, if she was completely honest.

Cole perked up. "Can they stay for dinner with us tomorrow night? You know Nate can't cook," he cajoled.

Knowing they had to stop acting as if they were a family, and get back to the reality of leading separate lives, at least part of the time, Brooke responded, "He's also very good at going to restaurants or picking up take-out meals."

Cole marched over to the computer, switched it on and regarded her glumly. "It's not the same thing as the four of us sitting down together."

Brooke missed the camaraderie, too. That wasn't the point. They'd had independent lives before they met; for all their sakes, they needed to set some boundaries and maintain them. "Cole, I know we felt like a family when we were there," she started awkwardly. *And that's my fault. I fell for the fantasy, hook, line and sinker.*

Hurt glimmered in Cole's eyes. "We *are* a family, Mom," he interrupted, a crestfallen expression on his face. "Or at least we could be if you weren't so stubborn!"

Maybe someday, Brooke thought wistfully. But only if she and Nate were in love. And although they had made love, and flirted with the idea of it, neither of them had begun to make that kind of no-holds-barred commitment. Until they did, she couldn't let Cole think more was possible. He'd already been disappointed enough in the personal realm.

Forcing herself to be practical yet again, when all she really wanted to do was be wildly impractical and impulsive, she counseled, "I know the last two weeks were fun, but right now we each need space to get back to our normal lives."

Cole scowled and stormed out of the room. "I don't want my normal life—I want a dad and a brother. I want Nate and Landry!"

HER SON'S WORDS still ringing in her ears, Brooke gave up sorting through the mail and went to take a shower. She wished she could give Cole what he wanted. But his reaction to leaving the mansion after just two weeks of interacting daily with Landry and Nate filled her with fear. She had a responsibility to prevent her son from being hurt by unrealistic expectations, as well as a duty to let Nate—who might be dealing with the same thing with Landry—know what was going on.

"I'm glad you called," Nate told her when he showed up on her doorstep at noon the following day.

Ignoring his warm, deliberate gaze and blatantly sensual manner, she stiffened her resolve and ushered him inside. "I wanted to talk to you when the boys weren't present." She had promised herself she was going to get their life back on track and return everything to normal. Actively taking steps to do so already made her feel stronger. "Since they're both at camp for the day, this was the perfect time." Mindful of his busy schedule, she led Nate into the living room.

He took off his suit jacket, draped it over the back of a wing chair and loosened the knot on his tie. "I wanted to talk to you, too. Landry moved into the main house last night after you left."

The announcement filled her with happiness. Brooke tore her eyes from the exposed column of Nate's throat, aware he'd been with her for less than a minute and her pulse was already pounding at his nearness. "That's great!" she said.

He grinned like a proud dad emerging from the delivery room. The words spilled out joyously. "I offered to move into the caretaker's cottage with him...since Landry was already comfortable there. But he said he thought it was time he started acting like he was my son—for real—and not just some guest."

Brooke wrapped Nate in a congratulatory hug, then stepped back, still smiling as she looked up at him. "That is big," she said warmly. "I am so happy for you."

He dipped his head in acknowledgment, then sobered. "The only problem is he misses you and Cole."

Empathy united them once again. "Cole feels the same way," she admitted.

Nate studied her through hooded eyes, leaving Brooke feeling as if they were suddenly on the verge of something even more compelling...and emotionally risky...

Her heart began to pound.

He curved a hand over her cheek and temple, and pushed away her hair. "Unless I'm wrong," he confessed, gazing reverently into her eyes, "I think we all miss each other."

Emotion welled inside Brooke, along with a longing unlike anything she had ever felt. Unable to help herself, she looked straight into his eyes and whispered, "You're not wrong. You're not wrong at all." And then she did what she had wanted to do ever since he walked in. She put aside what she knew she should do and leaned in to kiss him.

NATE HADN'T COME OVER to make love, but now that Brooke had issued the invitation, he was all for it. Filled with longing and the primal need to possess, he gathered her close. Cupping her face in his hands, he tilted her chin for better access. One kiss melted into another. She returned his passion, straining against him, her body undulating softly. Sensations hammered him. The hot heavy pressure in his groin nestled against her closed thighs. Knowing he had to find a way to be closer to her, to find the fulfillment they both sought, Nate lifted his head. "Your bedroom okay?"

She wreathed her arms about his neck and gazed up at him. "More than okay."

Nate needed no further persuasion. He swept her up into his arms and carried her down the hall to the master suite. He set her down next to her bed, then lowered his head to hers once again. Her lips parted and he swept his tongue inside her mouth, tasting the sweetness, and assuaging the desperate hunger inside him.

They undressed in a haze of longing. When they had finished, she looked up at him, her eyes glowing with love. And Nate knew his search was over. He had found the woman—the only woman—for him, at long last.

She guided him onto the lace-edged sheets that adorned her bed.

They kissed again, their caresses melting one into another. Brooke's body ignited in a flame of sensation. And she knew what she had been trying to deny for days now. There was no guarantee what the future held, and there never had been. The chance to be with Nate like this might be as fleeting as she feared in the darkest recesses of her soul. But if she didn't take advantage of it, right now, she would regret for the rest of her life not making love with him. And she didn't want any regrets where he was concerned. She wanted only love and sweet, wonderful memories that would sustain her when life was not so great, yet again….

Nate's hands skimmed lower, slipping between her

thighs. He explored her intimately, his questing caress sending her arching up into the warmth of his fingertips. He was hard all over, and lower still, below the waist, as aroused as she. She let her palm close around him, wanting to draw out the experience as sensually as possible, knowing she had never needed or wanted him more than at that moment.

"I don't want to be without you," he whispered, between deep, demanding kisses.

"I don't want to be without you, either," she confessed, as their bodies melded in boneless pleasure. Hers felt as if it were on fire from the inside out. Unable to wait any longer, she grasped his hips and guided him, so he was positioned precisely where he should be. Surrendering with a fierce, unquenchable ache, she murmured, "I want you. Now, Nate!"

"I want you, too." He kissed her again, commanding everything she had to give, then pushed her thighs apart with his knees. He stroked her gently and that was all it took. Brooke arched up from the bed, already falling apart, as he surged inside her. Overwhelmed with sensation, with the feelings welling in her heart, she let every part of her love every part of him, until at last they were soaring, flying free.

It was only hours later, as Nate dressed again and prepared to leave, that he noticed the message from his physician's office on his phone, asking him to call in immediately.

Chapter Fourteen

"You found out the results of the DNA test, didn't you?" Landry guessed, apprehension tautening the lines of his young face.

It was all Nate could do not to look at Brooke. He had asked her to be with him when he told Landry. In turn, Landry had asked that Cole be present. It seemed that everyone needed reinforcements for this "talk." And right now, Cole looked as tense and pale and out of his mind with worry as Landry.

Nate squared his shoulders and said the words he had hoped never to utter. "Our DNA did not match. You and I are definitely not father and son."

Landry's gangly shoulders sagged. "So Miles Lawrence is my dad, after all."

Although there was no way to say definitely, since Lawrence was deceased, Nate took it on faith. "It would appear so."

"Are they sure?" Landry leaned forward urgently in his seat, clasped hands dangling in front of him. The desperation to belong gleamed in his eyes. "I mean, I'm way more like you than I am him, at least what I know of him."

"It doesn't matter what the genetics are." Nate worked to quell his own disappointment. Strength and conviction were what was needed here. "I told you that before." He looked Landry in the eye. "I still want to be your dad. I want you to be my son."

The teen raked both his hands through his hair, despair pouring out of him. "It's not going to be the same," he muttered.

Nate clamped a paternal hand on his shoulder. "It'll be exactly the same," he assured him.

"How can you say that?" Landry demanded, jerking away.

Vaguely aware of the distraught looks on both Brooke's and Cole's faces, Nate followed him. "Because nothing of importance will change. The adoption is still going to go through."

Landry shook off both touch and reassurance once again. Refusing to look anyone in the eye, he pivoted. "I'm going outside." He dashed away and slammed out of Brooke's home.

Cole headed for the back door, too. "I'll talk to him," he threw the words over his shoulder.

Nate wasn't sure what Cole could say. Brooke looked as if she didn't know what to do or say, either. She was about to try when the doorbell rang. A glance through one of the transom windows beside the portal caused the color to leave her face. From where he stood, Nate couldn't see the visitor. "Who is it?"

"Professor Rylander."

Obviously, Nate thought, the English lit department had news, too.

Brooke looked to Nate to run interference. "The boys can't know he's here. I'll talk to him outside."

"I'll take care of it," Nate promised.

Trembling slightly, she opened the front door and eased out onto the porch, shutting the door behind her. While she was doing that, Nate noticed a United States Postal

Service truck pull up at the curb. A mailwoman got out, clipboard in hand, and headed up the walk. The uniformed courier stopped in front of Brooke, passed her a card for signature. She waited for Brooke to comply, then handed over a letter.

Phineas Rylander seemed to be urging Brooke to open it. She did, and paled even more.

Nate was torn between his role as sentry and that of protector.

Decision made, he started toward the front door. Only to have Brooke open it and slip through, certified letter in hand.

"What's going on?" he asked in concern.

"Professor Rylander wanted to let me know that the book party was canceled."

"How come?" Cole walked in to join them.

Landry was still outside, sitting on the back patio.

Brooke hesitated.

Cole's glance fell to the publisher's logo on the envelope in her hand. And suddenly, Nate realized, the do-or-die moment Brooke had been dreading was upon them.

IT WAS NOW OR NEVER, Brooke thought. Yet even as she opened her mouth to explain to Cole what was going on, she was torn with indecision. Should she destroy what little illusion her son had left? Or continue covering for Seamus to protect Cole, and wait until her son was much older to let him know the whole story? She had only seconds to decide. And in the end, she knew what she had to do.

Brooke looked her son in the eye and stuck to the facts she felt she could reveal to him at this time. "The publisher has decided not to go ahead with your father's last book."

Cole's brow furrowed in confusion. "How come?"

Her chest tightened. She knew what Nate would want her to do here. She knew he wouldn't respect her if she didn't come clean. But she wouldn't live up to his high standard of parenting. She still couldn't adhere to—or even agree with—his standard of parenting. "I'm not sure," Brooke fibbed finally. "But the publisher also told the university of their decision, so the party in your dad's honor has been canceled, too."

Cole's face crumpled. "This doesn't make sense!" he cried. "People love all that mushy stuff."

Brooke recalled taking Cole to a book signing when he was six. Seamus had been surrounded by fawning women and students who idolized him. But that had been when Seamus still had a seductively cheery outlook on life. "Well, that was part of the problem, honey. This new collection of poems was very dark, and there just…" She swallowed, aware she was about to tell an even bigger fib. "There isn't a market for it. Not the kind that's needed."

"Well, at least we've got the advance copy," Cole said. "In case we want to look at it someday."

Actually, Brooke thought, they didn't, as she had given that to the intellectual-property lawyer she'd hired to represent their interests. Unable to tell Cole any of that right now, however, she changed the subject to a matter even more pressing. "How's Landry?"

Cole's expression darkened. "Bummed."

Her heart swelled. "Can we do anything for him?" she asked.

Her son shook his head and averted his gaze to the backyard, where Landry was still hanging out, alone. "I think we're going to walk down to the park for a while, if it's okay."

Brooke looked at Nate for a decision.

He shrugged, then turned back to Cole. "Okay by me, if it'll help. You got your cell phone?"

Cole patted his pocket.

"Call if you need anything," Brooke advised.

"Okay." Cole went back outside, spoke to Landry. The taller teen stood, and together they headed out the back gate.

Feeling as if she had dodged yet another bullet, Brooke let out a long, slow breath. "What didn't you tell Cole?" Nate asked.

The simple question evoked a flood of guilt. Not trusting herself to speak, she handed over the letter.

Nate read it for himself. "...due to the fact that it cannot be established that Seamus Mitchell is the sole author and owner of this Work...and is at risk of legal claim, suit and/or action...Publisher is giving notice of its intention to cancel publication of the work. All advance monies paid to the Author's Estate are to be returned to the Publisher, within six months of this notification...as per the terms of the contract...." He put down the letter. "Is Iris Lomax going to sue?"

"So far all she has done is threaten. She's met with the university and their intellectual-property lawyers. And while they can't prove Seamus authored any of the poetry, even partially, any more than I can, they don't feel she has produced enough evidence of her own to actually prevail in civil court." Brooke sighed. "But just the publicity of the claim would be devastating to all concerned. Hence, the publisher's and the university's immediate move to permanently distance themselves from Seamus and anything he may or may not have done."

"Even so..." Nate shook his head, clearly worried. "You have to let Cole know what's going on."

As if it were only that easy, Brooke thought bitterly,

wishing she could have depended on Nate to support her in this very important regard. She threw up her arms in frustration. "I can't tell Cole his father is suspected of plagiarizing the work of a young woman he was having an affair with!"

Nate challenged her with the lift of his brow. "Better to let him find out some other way?"

The sarcasm stung. "I'll talk to my lawyer, have him come to some kind of settlement with Iris Lomax to keep her quiet."

Nate gave her a long look, his expression grave. "We have to be realistic here. Too many people know about it now for it to stay quiet indefinitely. If the Dallas or Fort Worth papers, or even faculty at of the competing universities in the area learn of this, the news will be public. You can't let Cole find out that way. You owe it to him to be honest with him."

Brooke knew they were at a turning point. Nate would either understand her point of view or he wouldn't. "My goal here is to protect him. To keep Cole from becoming disenchanted."

Nate shook his head in silent censure. "By lying to him, directly and by omission."

Brooke's knees felt as shaky as her moral center. "Whose side are you on?" she cried, upset.

"Yours."

She regarded Nate stonily, feeling as if her heart were encased in a block of ice. "It doesn't sound that way."

Nate picked up the paper and waved it impatiently. "If Cole finds out any of this, and realizes you knew and didn't tell him, he is going to be completely devastated. He's going to question whether or not he can ever trust you again."

Nate wasn't telling her anything she hadn't already

thought about—many times. Brooke knew this had the potential to destroy her relationship with her son. She didn't need Nate questioning her beliefs, making her doubt herself, the same way Seamus had done, time and time again. "I don't see that it helped Landry to know the truth," she countered, resolute.

Nate's eyes turned grim. "If you're referencing the DNA test—"

Brooke's lower lip trembled as she forced herself to assert, "Landry would have been better off if you had just denied that it was possible you could be his father."

Nate braced his hands on his waist. "I didn't have a choice once he saw that photo and realized that his mother was still engaged to me eight months before he was born."

Brooke lifted her chin. "You could have made something up, or… I don't know…"

Nate's jaw clenched. "I couldn't do that to him."

"He's suffering."

"We both are," Nate declared flatly. "But we'll get over it, because we dealt with each other and the situation honestly."

Brooke had never considered Nate a cockeyed optimist, until now. "And if you don't? If Landry remains distraught and confused…then what?"

"We'll figure out a way to make things better."

Silence fell between them, every bit as devastating as their words.

Brooke held up a hand. "I can't talk about this anymore."

He clamped a hand on her shoulder. "We have to."

She shrugged free, feeling as if her heart was breaking. "This is my decision to make, Nate," she reminded him, hanging on to her composure by a thread. "Your only job as my friend—" *and lover* "—is to back off and support whatever I decide."

"Listen to me, Brooke. I know what it is to be so devastated by just the thought of betrayal that you can't deal, because I did that with Seraphina. But burying your head in the sand and pretending a situation doesn't exist doesn't help anything. It only makes things worse." He looked her square in the eye. "As painful as it is, you have to start facing reality here and help Cole deal with his father's frailties."

Her spirits sank even lower. "That sounds like an ultimatum."

Nate stared at her, a force not to be denied. "I can't just stand by and do nothing while you put yourself and Cole in harm's way."

Brooke braced herself for the worst, even as she stipulated angrily, "You can't tell Cole, either."

Nate exhaled in displeasure. "I wouldn't have to. Your son is a smart kid. As time goes on, he'll figure it all out. And like I said…if it comes to that, he'll never trust you again."

Brooke's lower lip trembled. "You're supposed to back me up!"

But to her dismay, he refused. He moved toward her, his arms held out beseechingly. "If we're going to have a relationship that endures, we have to be able to talk about things and work them out, even when we disagree."

Brooke evaded his embrace and stalked past him. "What you really mean is that I have to do things your way." She whirled around to face him once again. "I've already been in a marriage like that. Where my husband belittled my opinions and made all the major decisions for us, and I had no choice but to follow. I won't do that again, either."

Nate rocked back on his heels. "You're deliberately misinterpreting."

She stomped closer. "And you're deliberately underplaying the significance of this argument! I can't be with someone who won't do everything in his power to protect my son."

Nate looked even more irritated. "And I can't be with someone who would willingly lie to her son, or mine."

There it was, the ultimatum she had been expecting all along. The one that told her...once again...she just wasn't good enough to hold the love and attention of the man she wanted.

Brooke worked to keep her emotions under wraps. "So it's over?" she asked with icy control.

Nate shrugged, no longer the hot-blooded lover she desired and once again the accomplished CEO who always walked off alone. "It has to be," he told her, in that crisp businesslike voice she knew so well. He exhaled in silent censure, shook his head, then once again met her eyes. "Thank God we didn't tell the kids there was ever anything going on in the first place."

Bitterness welled inside her. Brooke looked at Nate, feeling more disillusioned than ever before. "I can't argue with that."

Refusing to cry in front of him, she rushed toward the front door. "I'm going to go check on the boys." Once past Nate, she practically sprinted down the block.

He was right behind her, his long strides eating up the sidewalk. Brooke rushed on. She got to the small two-acre park in the middle of her subdivision. Two toddlers were playing on the swings with their mothers. A group of boys was playing pickup basketball. There was no sign of Cole or Landry.

Nate caught up with her, his strides as unhurried as

hers had been rushed. Hands clamped on his waist, pushing back the edges of his suit coat, he gazed around. "Is this where they're supposed to be?" he growled in frustration.

Brooke nodded, scanning the area, to no avail.

"Anywhere else they might have gone?"

Beginning to feel a little panicky, Brooke forced herself to concentrate. "I don't know. You ask the boys and I'll ask the two moms."

Nate and Brooke went their separate ways. When they returned to each other, her news was bad. Judging by the grim expression on Nate's face, so was his. "They were here, but they didn't play ball," he reported. "They went down to the corner and hopped on a city bus instead."

NATE DIALED LANDRY'S mobile-phone number. Brooke dialed Cole's. Neither answered. Frantic, Brooke checked her cell-phone messages, while Nate walked off to do the same.

She had one from the IP attorney, asking her to call. Apparently he'd heard about the book cancellation and the university's position, too. The second was an emotional entreaty from Cole. "You have to stop treating me like a kid, Mom, and start telling me what's really going on! 'Cause until you do—" his voice broke slightly before becoming defiant once again "—I'm not coming home!" *Click.*

Nate walked back toward Brooke. Trembling, she handed him her phone and had him listen to Cole's message.

He handed her his.

Landry's disconsolate voice sounded in her ear. "Look, Nate, I know you're trying to do the right thing here. You always do the right thing. But the truth is I'm not your kid. And that has to matter a lot more than you say. I know it does. So...you're off the hook," Landry choked out. "I'm outta here." *Click*.

"I can't believe this." Heart pounding, Brooke clutched the cell phone. "They've run away."

Nate put his emotions aside and focused on the problem. "They can't have gotten very far."

Maybe not, but... Brooke swallowed as a hundred horror stories crossed her mind. "You don't have to get very far from home for something bad to happen, Nate."

He grimaced and wrapped a reassuring arm around her shoulders. Determination lit his eyes. "We'll find them."

Brooke only wished she felt as sure. "How?" she asked, once again on the verge of breaking down.

Nate tightened his grip on her protectively before releasing her altogether. Heading back toward her house, he said, "Those phones I gave them are equipped with GPS. I didn't activate the feature. I didn't think we'd need to, but I'm sure as soon as the service provider turns it on, we'll know exactly where they are. Unfortunately, I'm going to have to go over to one of the stores in person to get that done."

At least they had a plan. Brooke was prepared to do her part, too. She pulled herself together, as she too raced toward her home, where their vehicles were parked. "While you do that, I'm going to start driving around the neighborhood, looking for them."

"Call me if you find them," he said, as he climbed into his Jaguar.

"I will," Brooke promised, before running inside to get her purse and car keys. "And you do the same."

Brooke checked out all Cole's favorite haunts. The burger place a mile and a half from home. The video store and the park. The strip mall and, farther away, the bigger retail shopping mall where they had gone to get clothes and haircuts.

While she searched, she called Cole on his cell phone every five or ten minutes, leaving another message, pleading with him to let her know where he was so they could talk this over. She also called a few of his close school friends. No one had heard from him.

As for Landry... He had no one she knew of to turn to...except... And suddenly, Brooke knew. She picked up her phone and dialed again. And found the answer she had been looking for.

NATE AND BROOKE MET UP in the parking lot of the retirement center. "Thank God they're safe," she said, aware she had never been happier to see him or be with him in her life. She needed Nate's love and support, and right now, even though she supposed they were still technically broken up, she could feel both exuding from him in waves.

Nate again wrapped a comforting arm around her shoulders.

Once again, Brooke noted, almost by default they were parenting their two boys together. But was it anything more than that? Could it ever be again? She didn't know the answer. The inscrutable expression on his handsome face gave her no clue. "Do any of them know that we're aware the boys are here?" Nate asked quietly.

Hoping the two of them still had a chance to make things right with each other, as well as their two sons, Brooke relinquished control and leaned on Nate's strength. "I asked the staff not to say anything to the boys or Jessalyn, just to keep them here until we arrived."

As they neared the entrance to the building, Nate dropped his arm and moved away from her. "Guess we should have come here first," he murmured, the brooding, serious CEO look back on his face.

Brooke's shoulders slumped. "Guess we should have done a lot of things." Treated Cole like the grown-up he was turning into, let him in on the problems, no matter how painful the process.

Without warning, Nate reached over and clasped her hand, one friend to another. He looked her in the eye. "We'll get through this."

With him by her side, Brooke felt they just might.

They walked into the center, signed in at the reception desk and then headed back to Jessalyn's private suite, where the boys were holding court with Landry's great-grandmother.

As Brooke and Nate walked in, both boys started guiltily, then just as quickly turned defiant. Cole clamped his arms across his chest and thrust his chin out stubbornly. "I'm not going home until you tell me the truth."

Jessalyn reached for her cane. "Perhaps I should let you-all talk alone," she said.

Landry held on to her arm. "No, Gran. Stay."

"He's right," Nate told her kindly. "You're family. And this is a family matter."

"I told Landry and Cole both they should not have run away," Jessalyn said, pausing to give her teenage callers a stern look. "As difficult as it can sometimes be, there are better ways to make a point."

"And the point of all this, for me, anyway—" Landry locked eyes with Nate "—is I am not your kid."

THIS WAS IT, Nate thought. His big chance to step up to the plate and figure out how to be the kind of father Landry deserved. There was no time to lean on Brooke to help bail him out, or to go to the guys for advice. It was his chance to be there emotionally for *his kid*—the way his parents had never been for him. And Landry was his kid. Nate had never been more sure of that. The question was how to convey it to him, to make him believe....

Nate pulled up a chair and sank into it so he and Landry were sitting face-to-face.

It was time, Nate thought, to dig deep—deeper than he had ever gone before—and speak straight from his gut. Because he was never going to get in the game the way he wanted to be, if he didn't risk his whole heart.

"While I don't agree with your actions today—and for the record, if you ever pull a stunt like this again, you're going to be grounded within an inch of your life." He shot a warning look in Landry's direction. "But that being said... your actions did serve a purpose. And that was to get my attention."

Nate held up a staying hand when Landry started to object. "Let me get this off my chest, okay?" He sighed. "The truth is, you were right—the DNA test *does* matter. I wanted us to be linked that way. In fact, I felt sure we were, because over the last few weeks I feel like we've truly become father and son. So it sure would have been nice to know we shared the same chromosomes." He paused for a long moment. "But even though the test didn't turn out the way we'd hoped, it will not ever change the way I feel about you."

"How can you say that?" Landry lamented, tears welling in his eyes.

"Because I love you, Landry. You are my family," Nate said emphatically. "We're father and son in every way that matters. And to make it real—to make it lasting—all we have to do is take the next step and make it legal." He paused, his heart in his throat. "So what do you say? I want to be your father from now on. But the question is do you want to be my son?"

Chapter Fifteen

Brooke could not stop crying and Landry hadn't even answered yet.

Nate was the best man—the best dad—she had ever had the privilege to know. Landry was one lucky kid. The question was, did he know it yet? Judging from the unchecked tears pouring down his face—and Nate's—they were both beginning to grasp the importance of this link they shared.

"Well, heck," Landry mumbled, crying openly now, "if you put it that way." The lanky teen stood and threw himself into Nate's arms. The lump in Brooke's throat grew, along with the joy in her heart.

"I'll call Ms. Tanous and get the legal stuff going first thing tomorrow morning," Nate said thickly, holding the boy tightly.

Landry nodded, and continued to weep, in joy and relief, while Cole watched with tearful longing.

Nate finally clapped Landry on the back. Dabbing their eyes, appearing a little embarrassed, the two stepped apart. Cole sat there, waiting. Obviously happy for his friend, yet more bereft than ever for himself. And Brooke knew it was time she stepped up to the challenge, too. In a way she had been avoiding.

She brought a chair over and sat opposite Cole, the way

Nate had done with Landry. Gently, she reached out and took her son's hand. She hated the resistance she felt from him, but she understood, and knew she deserved it. "You're right to be upset with me, Cole. I haven't been honest with you about what is going on, either."

"Why not?" he challenged, clearly angry now.

Brooke gulped and kept her gaze on him steady. "Because I was trying to protect you," she explained gently.

Cole's lip thrust out mutinously. "From what?" he demanded.

"The truth."

Silence fell between them. "This has something to do with that Iris Lomax person, doesn't it?" Cole asked emotionally.

It was Brooke's turn to be taken aback. "What do you know about that?"

"She was Dad's teaching assistant. She used to come over to the house sometimes when you weren't there." Cole explained. "They were writing poetry together—the poetry that was in Dad's new book."

Poetry that had detailed the suffocating confinement of marriage...countered by the joyous rebirth of passion. Her heart sank. Unsure whether she felt more humiliated or foolish, she asked, "You're sure they were doing it together?"

Cole shrugged, looking unbearably young again. "Well...from what I overheard...Ms. Lomax was coming up with most of the stuff, but Dad was the one who was saying it was either okay or not." Cole frowned. "You know how picky he was about words and stuff."

Yes, Brooke had known. Up to now, she had only thought that impacted Cole because his father had been too impatient and overbearingly critical to help his son with his homework. Had she been more attuned to what was going on, she surely would have seen Cole was upset about much more than that with his dad, in the months leading up to Seamus's untimely death. Instead, she had naively chalked it up to father-son angst.

Aware that Cole was waiting for her to explain, she forged on. "Well, that's been part of the problem that I didn't want you to know about. Ms. Lomax claims that your father stole that work from her. She says he wasn't the author of the poetry, that she was. As a result, the publisher had no choice but to stop publication of the book." Brooke exhaled softly. "If your dad was still here with us, it would be different. Because he isn't here to defend himself or explain whatever the writing process was that he and Ms. Lomax used, they can't be sure he didn't plagiarize her writing."

A cynical expression crossed Cole's face. He sat back in his chair with a disillusioned but accepting sigh. "I think he did, Mom. At least a little bit."

Given the extent of Seamus's writer's block, so did Brooke. "I've been thinking we may want to turn the rights for the material over to Iris Lomax, let her publish it under her name, or her name and Dad's," Brooke said.

"I think we ought to just give the stuff to her, Mom, and leave Dad out of it," Cole said.

"I think you're right," Brooke agreed. It would make so many of their problems go away. "Morally, it's the right thing to do." And legally, and financially... "Anyway, that is why the university canceled the party—because there is no new book to celebrate," she finished.

Cole looked her in the eye. Something still seemed to be troubling him, she noted, and the continued wariness in his expression made her heart sink. He was still looking at her as if he thought she had betrayed him on some level. Obviously, they hadn't aired all their troubles yet. She waited for him to tell her what was on his mind.

Finally, Cole blurted, "Did Dad have an affair with Ms. Lomax?"

Another stab to the heart. Not for the infidelity—Brooke had long ago come to terms with that—but for the fact that her son had to suffer the pain of the betrayal, too. Careful only to deal with what her son was old enough to handle, she asked, "Do you even know what that is?" She hadn't covered it in her sex talk with him, and neither had the school….

Cole rolled his eyes, then sighed. "Mom, I'm thirteen, not ten! Yes, I know what that is! It's when two people who aren't married sleep together and stuff."

Brooke's defenses went up. Apparently she wasn't as good at this truth-telling as Nate was yet. She studied her son. "Why would you think they had an affair?" It broke her heart that she and Cole were forced to have this conversation.

He shoved his chair back several inches and stared at her with adolescent angst, commanding her to treat him like the adult he deemed himself to be. "Because that night at the hospital, when I went there to see Dad in the CCU, I heard some of the nurses talking about how horrible it was that he'd been with that grad student when he died, instead of his wife. It sounded like…" Cole choked.

"He and that Iris lady were in bed," Landry interjected for him.

Cole sent him a grateful glance, then turned back to his mom.

She didn't know what to say.

Cole continued, more composed now. He seemed determined to get this all out. "And that wasn't really a big surprise, because he was always flirting with Iris Lomax when she came to the house." He gulped. "And I saw him kissing her a few times." Bitterness mingled with the confusion and hurt on Cole's young face. "He told me not to tell you, and I didn't because I didn't want to hurt you, but…it made me mad, seeing him do that with her. It wasn't right for him to cheat on you like that…."

No, it hadn't been.

The worse thing, Brooke thought with a stab of guilt that went soul-deep, was that Cole had been forced to carry this burden alone for several years. Her own body sagged miserably before she reached out to touch his arm. "You should have told me what you'd seen."

Visibly confused, he shrank from her touch. "I couldn't. I didn't want to hurt *you*."

And yet, Brooke thought, even more miserably, they had both done that anyway, despite their best intentions.

Cole sized her up. "But you were already hurt, weren't you?"

"Yes," Brooke noted sadly. "As were you."

Cole waited. Brooke knew she had to say something that would help her son put this all in perspective. But what? She turned to Nate. He gave her an encouraging glance, and suddenly she knew what she had to do was put it all out there, and let the chips fall where they may.

"Yes, your father had an affair with Ms. Lomax. I didn't know about it until the night he died, and I found out then by accident, same as you." She took a deep breath and forced herself to go on. "I had hoped you would never learn about it. I didn't want you to think less of your father…." *But instead you ended up thinking less of me.* Brooke felt like a total failure as a mother. "So I covered for him."

This, Cole already knew.

His jaw clenched. "Were you ever going to tell me?"

The fifty-million-dollar question. Once again, she forced

herself to dig deep and answer honestly. "I don't know. But I should have told you at least the part you could handle at the time. Because if I had done that it would have opened the door for you to confess to me all you had seen and heard." She sighed with regret. "You wouldn't have had to carry these secrets for all these years, and neither would I. And that would have been better for both of us, I think."

Cole relaxed, at ease once again. He regarded her with forgiveness in his eyes. "Yeah," he told her gravely, "it would have."

Brooke reached across and clasped both his hands in hers. "I'm sorry I made a mistake." She squeezed his palms with all the mother love she had to offer and looked him straight in the eye. "I promise you I won't do it again. If something bad happens, I'll tell you right away. And I want you to do the same with me."

Cole's eyes welled, even as the love poured out of him. "I will...I promise," he said thickly.

Her own eyes misting over, even as relief poured through her, Brooke stood and held out her arms. Cole went into them, and they hugged each other fiercely.

Finally, Cole stepped back. "There's only one more thing we want to know," he told his mother bluntly. He turned and looked at Landry.

Whatever the two young men were thinking, Brooke noted, they were totally on the same page.

Landry nodded, and Cole pivoted back to Brooke and Nate. He took a deep breath and said, "Me and Landry want to know what's going on with the two of you."

Cole paused a beat, and wordlessly, Landry urged him on, as only an older brother could. Then Cole demanded even more bluntly, "Do you love Nate, Mom? And does Nate love you?"

OUT OF THE MOUTHS of teens, Brooke thought, as her heart kicked inside her chest.

Did they love each other? Brooke knew how she felt, notwithstanding their recent disagreement. But how did he feel? Was it enough? Should they even be discussing this? Especially now, when so much had already been disclosed.

With a mixture of relief and apprehension, she realized that Nate apparently thought so. His posture CEO-confident, he closed the distance between them and took her hand. She searched his eyes, still not knowing what lay ahead, almost afraid to wish....

His expression inscrutable, Nate spoke to Cole, Landry and Jessalyn. "It's a good question. And I'm going to answer it, but I need a moment to speak with your mother privately first."

Jessalyn smiled, a matchmaker's gleam in her eyes.

Cole's glance narrowed speculatively, as did Landry's.

The next thing Brooke knew, Nate had placed a cordial hand beneath her elbow. Gallantly, he escorted her from the room and down the hall, past the groups gathered in the solarium, to the deserted patio outside. As she swung around to face him, her heart rate kicked up another notch. Never had she hoped for so much.

"First, I owe you an apology," Nate said.

Was that all this was? A chance to clear the air before going back to tell everyone that although they had briefly tested the waters, they were going to be "just friends"?

Brooke knew only that she didn't want to squander what chance of happiness she had left. Still holding Nate's steady gaze, she swallowed the knot of emotion in her throat. "I owe you one, too."

A corner of his mouth kicked up ruefully. "You knew

the whole DNA thing was more emotionally complicated than I was willing to let it be."

She nodded. "And you knew I should have leveled with Cole all along, that pain is as much a part of life as joy. And as much as we want to, we can't shield our children from pain." Feeling as if her whole soul had been laid bare, Brooke joked nervously, "Put our two methods together and we would almost be the perfect parent."

Nate chuckled, and she continued self-effacingly, "Minus another half-million mistakes along the way."

He sobered, suddenly looking as if his whole future was on the line, too. "I'm beginning to think it might be okay to let this idea of perfectionism go, at least when it comes to families and relationships."

Praying this wasn't a prelude to his giving up on them, Brooke went very still. She swallowed. "What are you saying?"

"My family was run like a business commodity when I was growing up."

Brooke knew Nate was insecure in his ability to connect with family the way loved ones should. He wasn't the only one who had come up missing. "I never had a dad." Never knew what a male role model in the home should be…until she'd seen Nate in action.

He compressed his lips together ruefully. "When it comes to relationships—the idea of marriage…kids—I don't have a clue what I'm doing."

At last, something in common, something to build on again. She took in a nervous breath, stepped closer and splayed her hands across the solid warmth of his chest. "Here's a secret. A lot of times I don't, either."

His hands settled around her waist. "But I know one thing, Brooke."

Beneath her fingertips, his heart was beating very hard and fast. Almost as quickly as her own, in fact.

"My life is better and a heck of a lot more satisfying with you in it."

Hope rushed through her, followed swiftly by an overwhelming tide of emotion. "My life is better, too," she whispered, misting up. "Way better, as Cole and Landry would say."

Nate nodded, ever so solemn and truthful and determined. "And that's why we have to throw in the towel, surrender our pride and admit we both lost the battle to keep it casual days ago," he finished in a rusty-sounding voice.

Brooke took a deep breath, braced herself. More nervous than ever, she asked, "You want to tell the boys we're dating?" She realized she was finally sure enough of her own feelings to take that leap.

"No," Nate said, in the flat decisive voice that said his mind was already made up. "We should have done that a while ago. Since we didn't..." He paused and searched her eyes. "Cole and Landry have been very clear that they want more than that from us. They want us to be a family."

Brooke's heart sank as the declaration she had been hoping to hear fell short. "I know that," she replied quietly. *I want that, too.* "But we can't continue to join forces just to fulfill some sort of fantasy the boys have of what their life would be like if we all stay together. Especially when we just promised them they would have the whole truth from both of us from here on out." Although what that was, on Nate's part, she *still* didn't know.

His grip on her tightened. "And it's a vow I mean to deliver on," he said in a tone that made her feel safe and protected.

The pulse in his throat was throbbing.

"Which is why I have to tell you what I should have told you days ago." Nate paused again and looked deep into her eyes, his expression raw, and filled with the longing she harbored deep inside. "I don't just want you or need you or want to spend every waking minute with you." He paused, then continued thickly, "Although for the record, all of that is true."

"For me, too." Brooke's own voice broke slightly.

Nate flashed a crooked smile. "That's good to hear," he told her reverently. "Because I love you, Brooke, with everything I am and everything I have. I love you more than I've ever loved anyone in my life."

Relief filtered through her, followed swiftly by joy. She threw her arms around his neck, brought him close and whispered tenderly, "Oh, Nate!" She was thrilled to realize she was finally getting everything she had ever dreamed. "I love you, too," she cried, trembling. She drew back and looked deep into his eyes. "So very much."

He gathered her even closer, bent his head and kissed her with the promise of all the days and nights to come.

Finally, he bussed her on the forehead and declared with typical CEO efficiency, "Then there is only one thing for us to do."

Epilogue

One year later...

"What did you say to the boys?" Brooke emerged from the bedroom dressed in a knee-length white silk dress. She watched as Landry and Cole raced away from the caretaker's cottage, showing the same energy and excitement with which they had dashed in.

"My credo, since I met you." Nate strode toward her, looking resplendent in his own light summer suit and tie. He took her hands in his and leaned forward to tenderly kiss her lips. "Slow and steady wins the race every time."

Brooke tingled from the caress. Holding on to Nate, she gazed up at him affectionately. The last year had been the happiest of her life, and the future looked even brighter. "Did they listen?"

His eyes sparkled with merriment. "Let's just say they're still intent on making a few 'miracles' of their own, via a surprise or two."

Curiosity mingled with the overwhelming excitement deep inside her. "Of which you know...?"

"Nothing," he confirmed, wrapping his arms around her. "I'll be as amazed by whatever they've dreamed up for us as you will be."

Brooke cuddled close and laid her cheek against his shoulder. Suffused with his warm, hard strength, she murmured, "The two of them are so sweet, to be putting on a small, private wedding for us."

It *was* an amazing gift, Nate thought.

All he and Brooke had had to do was okay the budget for the celebration and put them in touch with Jack's wife, wedding planner Caroline Mayer Gaines. The rest had been done, to the astonishment of all their friends, primarily by the two teenage boys. Now, he and Brooke—who had no superstitions about seeing each other prior to the ceremony—were sequestered together, awaiting their cue that it was time to get the show on the road.

Nate watched as Brooke went over to her jewelry case and removed the diamond necklace and earrings he had gifted her with the previous Christmas.

He helped her with the clasp of her necklace, while they continued talking about the wedding.

"Although as far as Cole and Landry are concerned," she reminded him with a teasing look, "we gave them no choice."

That was true, Nate thought. Both boys had vehemently vetoed Nate and Brooke's original plan to have their wedding ceremony in a judge's chamber, just down the hall from the courtroom where the adoption of both boys had become official that very morning. Now, Cole was officially Nate's son, and Landry was legally the son of Brooke as well as Nate. With Brooke and Nate's wedding, the circle would be complete and everyone would at long last have the loving family they had wanted.

"The kids wanted us to have a honeymoon. And we wanted to have the adoption on the first anniversary of the day we all met."

Brooke smiled and nodded. "It's all working out."

Cole raced back in. "Hey, Mom, you look great! You, too, Nate! Jessalyn and her friends from the retirement center have arrived!"

Landry was right behind him. "The rest of your friends and the judge are all here, too. So as soon as the sound team is done setting up, we're ready to go."

"Any clue what the music is going to be?"

Cole and Landry looked at each other and grinned. Cole said, "We figure when you hear it, you'll recognize it," he replied. "Nate, you will lead the way down the aisle. Landry is your witness, so he'll follow you. I'll go next, since I'm the official witness for Mom, and Mom...you're the bride—and the main attraction—so you'll go last."

Cole and Landry slipped outside.

A moment later, they came back in. Cole handed Brooke a beribboned bouquet of Texas wildflowers.

The strains of the famous Goo Goo Dolls song, "Let Love In"—a favorite of both Brooke and Nate—started up. The teens passed Brooke and Nate each a pair of dark sunglasses. "You're going to want these." They grinned, sliding on their own shades, then led the way out of the caretaker's cottage, onto the lawn. And together, the four of them danced and celebrated their way toward the guests....

"THIS IS ONE FANTASTIC wedding," Grady McCabe mused, several hours later, as the party wound on.

Dan grinned. "Foosball and Ping-Pong." He looked toward the sport court, where a tournament for the young people was set up and a wildly good time was being had by all.

Jack sipped champagne. "A wedding cake in the shape of your mansion. And a groom's cake that looks like the caretaker's cottage."

Nate shrugged. "A great sentimental choice by the boys, since this is where it all happened." Where he and Brooke fell in love, and Landry and Cole bonded. Where he'd become a father for the first—and second—time. And they all became the family they wanted and needed.

Travis slapped him on the shoulder as a radiant Brooke headed toward them. "Looks like you've got it all, Nate."

Nate's glance encompassed the loved ones of his four best friends, then turned back to them. Two years ago, they'd all been single. Now, they were all happily married. "We all do."

The guys murmured in agreement.

Brooke slipped her arm through Nate's. "The dancing is about to start."

Nate knew the kids had picked out the music for this, too. "Any idea what our song is going to be this time?"

"All I know is it's a slow tune. And very romantic. At least in their view."

"That's all I need to know." Nate winked at Brooke, then turned to the guys. "Excuse us, fellas. I've got a date to dance with the love of my life."

* * * * *

A sneaky peek at next month...

Cherish™

ROMANCE TO MELT THE HEART EVERY TIME

My wish list for next month's titles...

In stores from 21st October 2011:

❏ The Secretary's Secret — Michelle Douglas

❏ Rodeo Daddy — Soraya Lane

❏ Tall, Dark, Texas Ranger — Patricia Thayer

❏ Once Upon a Christmas Eve — Christine Flynn

❏ The Best Laid Plans — Sarah Mayberry

In stores from 4th November 2011:

❏ Thunder Canyon Homecoming — Brenda Harlen

❏ A Thunder Canyon Christmas — RaeAnne Thayne

❏ Baby Under the Mistletoe — Jamie Sobrato

Available at WHSmith, Tesco, Asda, Eason, Amazon and Apple

Just can't wait?

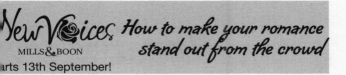

New Voices

MILLS & BOON

arts 13th September!

How to make your romance stand out from the crowd

voiding the dreaded cliché

en your story book with a bang—hook your reader in on the page and show them instantly that this story is unique.

uccessful writer can use a conventional theme and twist it deliver something with real wow factor!

ce you've established the direction of your story, bring in sh takes and new twists to these traditional storylines.

re are four things to remember:

- Stretch your imagination
- Stay true to the genre
- It's all about the characters—start with them, not the plot!
- M&B is about creating fantasy out of reality. Surprise us with your characters, stories and ideas!

whether it's a marriage of convenience story, a secret baby me, a traumatic past or a blackmail story, make sure you d your own unique sparkle which will make your readers ne back for more!

od luck with your writing!

e look forward to meeting your fabulous heroines and p-dead gorgeous heroes!

or more writing tips, check out:
www.romanceisnotdead.com

Visit us Online

NEWVOICESTIPS/B

Have Your Say

You've just finished your book.
So what did you think?

We'd love to hear your thoughts on our
'Have your say' online panel
www.millsandboon.co.uk/haveyoursa

- 🌹 Easy to use
- 🌹 Short questionnaire
- 🌹 Chance to win Mills & Boon®
  goodies